Skeletons, Secrets & Speakeasies

A Willowcroft Cozy Mystery Book Two

Fran Heap

First published by Frances Heap contactable at fran@franheapwriter.com

ISBN: 978-0-6457056-8-3   (paperback)

ISBN: 978-0-6457056-9-0   (ebook)

A catalogue record for this book is available from the National Library of Australia

Cover design by 100Covers.

Created with Atticus

"But flaws exist everywhere.
People make mistakes.
Buildings have weak points.
Stories have loose threads."
—Tammy Rumbelow

Chapter 1

"You know, they never found the money from the bank heist."

Xander's words ricocheted through Tammy Rumbelow's mind like a pinball, striking every corner of her imagination since he said them yesterday.

Could we actually find it?

They'd already solved the seventy-year-old locked room murder of Mary Collins—right there in what was now Tammy's living room.

Max Cross had killed her and hidden in a narrow space beside the fireplace to avoid getting caught.

Compared to that, tracking stolen cash seemed reasonable.

Not exactly what she'd expected when she moved to Willowcroft from LA for her fresh start.

The Swinging Spoon's neon sign cast a warm glow across their booth as Tammy stirred her milkshake. Vintage vinyl crackled from the jukebox, competing with the sizzle of bacon on the griddle and the richness of fresh-brewed coffee. Their ragtag detective team—Wally, Mrs. Hazel Temperance, Olivia, Xander, and Lockie the cat—huddled around the Formica tabletop.

If this were a scene in one of her novels, Tammy would have described it as "a clandestine meeting of unlikely allies." Her fingers itched for her notebook, but she forced herself to stay present. Real-life detection required more than clever turns of phrase.

"Makes you wonder," Xander leaned forward, elbows planted on the table. "If Max killed Mary to cover up his bank heist, what happened to the money? Did he spend it, or is it still tucked away somewhere in town?"

Mrs. Temperance's fingers disappeared into Lockie's fur, scratching behind his ears as he settled on Olivia's lap beside her. "Money doesn't just vanish."

Wally's forehead creased. "But the sheriff turned the town upside down and even neglected a murder investigation looking for it. If there was a stash, wouldn't they have found it?"

"Max was cunning," Olivia said. "If he squeezed into that concealed hole beside Tammy's fireplace and left the murder weapon there, there's no telling what else he did."

"Exactly!" Xander's eyes glinted. "I bet if we did some digging, we'd find where Max hid the loot. He lived within Greater Willowcroft his whole life. It has to be close by."

Tammy took another sip of her milkshake, savoring the cold sweetness complementing the warm pie on her plate. A late-night marathon to finish her first cozy mystery manuscript had left her with the particular brain fog of living too long in fictional worlds.

Ironically, her manuscript ended with the sleuth recovering stolen cash. Was her art imitating the life she might soon be living? Her stomach tightened. What if she was better at writing mysteries than solving them? Tammy pushed the thought away and focused on the comforting flavors dancing on her tongue, anchoring herself in the moment.

"With Max's recent passing, any details about the robbery likely died with him." She traced her finger around the rim of her plate, gathering a smudge of cinnamon. "But it would be fascinating to investigate."

Lockie meowed from Olivia's lap. Tammy recognized that calculated posture: tail twitching, body tense, every whisker angled toward the syrup-drenched pancakes. His single-minded determination was unmistakable.

If only she channeled such focus into her own plotting sessions instead of second-guessing every chapter, every word choice, every character motivation. Tammy took another bite of pie, letting the aromatic warmth of apple and spice soothe away the familiar spiral of self-doubt.

"Then it's settled," Olivia declared, guarding her plate from the cat's persistent paw. "Our next adventure will be finding the stolen money."

Nods circled the table.

"I've cleared the murder board, so we'll have a clean slate to work with." Olivia tilted her head. "Is it still called that if we're investigating a bank heist?"

"We can call it an investigation board," Tammy said, then snorted. "Though with our luck, we might add a murder or two before we're done."

"I'm calling it a murder board," Olivia grinned. "After all, we're investigating the death of the case, aren't we?"

The group groaned at her pun, but the corners of Olivia's eyes crinkled with delight.

Xander's fingers drummed against the tabletop. "Where do we start?"

"The library," Mrs. Temperance suggested.

Wally stroked his chin. "We should check the newspapers to ensure we have every article ever written about it."

"I have the ones I found when researching Mary Collins's murder," Xander said, "but I don't have them all. The archives of the Willowcroft Tribune and Gazette are in the library."

Olivia glanced at her watch. "I'll have to open the bookstore for Sunday afternoon hours soon. Several hikers from this morning said they'd be back after their trek. You can call me with genealogy leads I can work on between customers. Once you're done, come to the back room and start the board."

"Of course, dear," Mrs. Temperance—or Mrs. T, as they had begun affectionately calling her—replied. "You take care of your store, and we'll bring our findings to you."

Tammy studied the faces around the booth. Her new friends had become family in the wake of catching both a murderer and an attempted murderer in Max's grandson, Nathan, who targeted his own great-aunt, Eleanor.

Each brought unique skills to the table. Wally had a sharp eye honed through years as both a Boston homicide detective and Willowcroft's former sheriff. Xander, a tech-obsessed teen with more brains than social skills, was spending his summer break helping solve crimes instead of dodging them in online games.

Mrs. T had deep roots in the town and connections to every gossip mill, thanks to the Willow-Crafters knitting circle and her near-daily visits to Mrs. Hubbard's Cupboard, the town grocery store. And Olivia, part genealogist, part literary sleuth, could trace someone's great-aunt twice removed while recommending the perfect mystery novel, all without missing a beat behind the counter at Bookworm Haven.

The team filed out, the summer sun blasting their faces as they stepped onto the sidewalk.

Olivia gave Lockie one last scratch before handing him to Tammy. "You two be good now," she said, then headed next door to open her store, Bookworm Haven.

Tammy herded her friends across the sun-drenched square to the library. She guided them past the shelves of aged newspapers and documents, their musty scent triggering the thrill of plotting a new novel. They claimed a table and piled it high with records.

"We know Max Cross got away with the 1954 bank heist," Wally said, hunching forward. "But we don't know how."

"Right," Mrs. T agreed. "We need to find out more about Max and Willowcroft at the time. There must be something we've overlooked, a clue to how he did it and where he might have stashed the money."

Wally rubbed his hands. "Let's get to work." His fingers found Lockie's ears, eliciting a rumbling purr. "We'll find the lost money, won't we, buddy?"

Wally opened the bound *Willowcroft Gazette* newspapers on the table, Xander opened his laptop, Mrs. T disappeared into the stacks, and Tammy headed to the microfilm machines to start with the *Willowcroft Tribune*.

They had the exact date from researching Mary Collins's murder—which occurred three weeks after the heist. Two unsolved cases from seventy years ago, now connected. They'd proven Max Cross had murdered Mary, but he died before they could question him. The assumption was that Mary was killed because she knew about Max's involvement in the heist and refused to leave town. They never recovered the money, and Max never lived lavishly, so where was it?

He'd lived in Greater Willowcroft his entire life and died at Serenity Gardens Nursing Home a few weeks ago—the night before they planned to confront him.

Tammy scrolled through film reels until she reached the date of the heist. She squinted at the headline: "Bank Robbed, Thousands Stolen."

She pressed print and continued capturing every related article before collecting the copies and carrying them to the team's table.

"This article says over $300,000 was stolen." She slid the paper toward the center.

Xander's fingers flew across his keyboard. "Over three and a half million dollars today!"

Tammy read aloud, summarizing how the thief had slipped in and out with the money without being seen or leaving evidence.

"No leads, no suspects," Wally muttered.

"This article interviews the bank manager. He was distraught and puzzled, stating it was the first burglary in the bank's fifty years."

"Look at this!" Mrs. T hurried toward them from the stacks. "I took a different approach and researched the bank's history. I found an article from the day the bank opened in 1901."

The team clustered around her as she continued, "It describes the facade, the main banking hall, and even the basement vault. They invited towns-folk to inspect the vaults before opening."

A basement vault. Tammy squinted at the photograph of the proud stone facade, her writer's mind imagining.

Xander whistled low. "Can you imagine seeing the vault for the first time? Says here the door weighed over ten tons."

"It's impossible to break in without inside help," Tammy said, unable to tear her eyes from the picture.

"There's more." Mrs. T's smile spread across her face as she presented a color brochure. "The bank's centennial was in 2001. It says they added a mezzanine level in 1963 for more office space. The extra floor didn't exist when the robbery happened in '54."

"Good find, Mrs. T!" Tammy glanced between the brochure and the team. "So the upper level couldn't have played any part in Max's entry or exit."

Xander's jaw dropped as he stared at Mrs. T. "How did you find all this so quickly?"

Mrs. T chuckled. "I thought if I wanted to find old things, I should use the old catalog. And the card catalog drawers weren't empty like I'd assumed all these years. One card gave me everything I needed."

"I can't believe they kept the cards," Wally said.

Mrs. T nodded with pride. "Sometimes the old ways are the best."

A movement caught Tammy's eye—Lockie had abandoned his usual dignified perch and was pawing at something near Mrs. T's feet. Perfect cat timing, as always. Just when they needed a clue, their feline detective drew attention to exactly what they needed.

"Ah, yes. I also found the original blueprints of the bank."

"Let's take a look," Xander said.

"The library's closing in 10 minutes," called Maxine, the librarian, from the front desk.

Mrs. T sighed. "The library has such short hours on Sundays."

"Quick, let's check it out," Tammy urged.

They unfurled the brittle blueprints across the table. The inner workings of the building materialized before them.

Three and a half million dollars in today's money. A perfect robbery with no suspects. No wonder it had captured her imagination. The writer in her admired the elegance of the heist, while her newfound detective instincts buzzed with anticipation as she studied the blueprints.

"I'll take photos in sections so we can stick them together and study them later." Xander snapped away at the oversized drawing while the others jotted notes or made copies of their own discoveries.

Xander snatched his laptop from the table and dashed toward the exit. "I hope Olivia has Scotch tape!"

Chapter 2

Tammy, Mrs. T, and Wally crossed the square at a leisurely pace. *What will the blueprints show?*

The bell announced their arrival at the bookstore with a cheerful jingle. Olivia popped up from behind the counter like a jack-in-the-box, startling Tammy out of her thoughts.

"My tape dispenser has disappeared," Olivia said, patting the space beside the register. "It always sits right here. I had to give Xander a spare roll instead. He's printed something that needs assembling."

Mrs. T hung back. "Has Betty been in today, dear?"

Something in Mrs. T's voice made Tammy linger. The older woman's shoulders tensed, and her fingers tightened on her bag strap. *What's that about?*

"Yes, she was here before I closed for lunch," Olivia replied. "She was dying to read the next book in her romance series after finishing the previous one last night."

"I see." Mrs. T bit her bottom lip, the tiny gesture loaded with unspoken meaning.

There's a story there. Tammy filed the interaction away for later examination. They had a bank heist to solve.

"Oh well. It will turn up," Olivia said, breaking the moment. "Let's join the others."

She led them through the door to the back room disguised as a bookshelf nestled between the esoteric and true crime sections.

Xander had spread the printed photos across the table, his hands smoothing the edges. Wally cut tape beside him, his movements precise and methodical.

Mrs. T sank into her comfy chair, knitting needles already clicking, while Olivia bustled about getting iced tea and glasses.

Xander smoothed the map, tracing his finger along the lines. "The main vault was in the basement, accessed through the lobby. No windows, no other doors. One narrow hallway led downstairs." He leaned against the table. "There are no obvious vulnerabilities in the design. No secret tunnels or passages noted."

Olivia's look sliced through the room, dry and sharp, the same one Tammy had seen countless times when someone asked about Pride and Prejudice sequels.

"Did you think there was going to be a big 'X' marking the spot?" Olivia asked.

"It would have been nice," Xander shrugged.

That would make for terrible plotting. Too easy. The real world doesn't provide convenient markers.

Wally sighed. "How did Max get in and out with the cash?"

Tammy chewed the end of her pen. *Think methodically.* "Let's go over what we know about the layout in 1954. We have the lobby, the basement vault..."

"Don't forget the safety deposit box rooms," Mrs. Temperance said. "I have a box. It's in the vault."

"I bet there's buried treasure in there," said a grinning Xander.

Mrs. Temperance swatted his arm. "Oh hush, you."

Tammy scanned the blueprints. *Every story has its clues if you look hard enough.* Her finger traced the outline of the vault. "Everything seems to check out. The vault door and walls are solid concrete and steel. No ductwork big enough to wiggle through." She paused. "Could the basement have a hidden entrance?"

"Unlikely," Mrs. T replied. "Vaults were designed to be impenetrable—any extra entrances would have been a major security flaw."

But flaws exist everywhere. People make mistakes. Buildings have weak points. Stories have loose threads.

Wally's fingers drummed an impatient rhythm against the table. "Then how did Max get in and out without being seen?"

Xander shook his head. "Beats me."

"We're not giving up," Tammy said. "There's got to be something we missed."

She traced her finger over the blueprints again. *Front entrance... lobby... teller windows... Every mystery has a solution. I just need to find the right angle.*

"Only one entrance." Wally's finger pointed at the staircase leading to the vault.

"Windows?" Olivia suggested, peering over Tammy's shoulder.

Xander shook his head. "The ground-floor windows are too small. Maybe for a cat burglar." His gaze flicked to Lockie, who stretched on the table as if considering a career change.

Tammy smirked. "You mean a burglar with whiskers and an attitude."

Xander tapped the map. "How about the windows on the second floor?" His finger hovered over a large set of windows. "They're above the main banking hall."

"Too risky," Mrs. T replied. "Max would have had to climb up and down the exterior wall, which would have been far too visible."

Tammy shook her head. "Especially with the Sheriff's Department right next door. He'd have been spotted in seconds." *No criminal would be that obvious, not even in my worst first drafts.*

"And he would have needed a second long ladder inside with the mezzanine floor not being there," she added. *This isn't adding up. Max wasn't superhuman.* "He had to have an accomplice on the inside. Someone to let him in and out without raising suspicion."

"Possible," Wally conceded.

"Wait a minute." Mrs. Temperance squinted at the blueprints. "Do these show the deposit box numbers within each vault room?"

"Yes," Xander said, pointing to various sections. "These numbers correspond to the deposit boxes. For example, this room has boxes 1 to 150."

Mrs. Temperance's expression sharpened. "My father's box was 252, in the third room. I remember walking past the first two rooms as a child. The middle room always appeared more cramped than my current box, number 118, which is in the first room. Yet, on the map, all three rooms are marked the same size."

A discrepancy. Tammy's instincts tingled.

"Are you sure, Mrs. T?" Olivia asked.

"I accompanied my father to the bank regularly. I always noticed how shallow it was compared to the others we passed."

"Doesn't everything look smaller when we grow up?"

Not always. Some childhood memories are etched in stone.

"Has the bank remodeled the vaults?" Xander asked.

"Perhaps," Mrs. T conceded.

Tammy studied the map, her finger finding the inconsistency. "You're right, Mrs. T. This room has far fewer deposit boxes than the others, yet it's drawn as if it's the same size."

"Are the boxes bigger in there?" Olivia asked.

"No," said Mrs. T. "The bank has always maintained they are one size fits all."

Space doesn't disappear. Something else must be taking it up.

Xander sat back. "Are you telling me Max Cross knew of two hiding places in Willowcroft that allowed him to commit a murder and rob a bank?"

"But how would Max have known about something not on the blue-prints?" Olivia asked.

Good question. "Did Max work at the bank?" Tammy suggested, though even as she said it, she doubted it.

"He worked for his dad's construction company," Wally replied. "He doesn't strike me as someone who would have worked two jobs."

"Maybe Cross Construction Company did a remodel for them, like at my cottage," said Tammy. "History shows he doesn't mind tight spaces. Even a small passage wouldn't have been a problem for him."

This fits. This makes sense. Her excitement bubbled.

"He snuck in during daylight hours and hid until after dark," Olivia said.

"But how did he get the money and himself out?" Mrs. T asked.

Tammy's bubble deflated. "It only works if the space leads to another entrance." She slumped in her chair.

Silence settled over the room.

"I say we head to the bank and search for ourselves," said Tammy. *No amount of theorizing can replace firsthand investigation.*

"Oooh, we can use me as a decoy wanting access to my box," Mrs. T offered.

Xander clapped his hands. "An excursion to the Willowcroft Bank it is."

Mrs. Temperance stood. "I want to see if my childhood memories yield any more clues."

Olivia remained seated. "Are you all forgetting something?"

Everyone stopped and turned to her.

"For one, it's Sunday and the bank is closed, and two, the bank's building was subdivided further five years ago. That far-right deposit box room is now the recording studio for the Waves of Willowcroft radio station."

Of course it is.

Olivia turned to Tammy, and they spoke in sync: "A puzzle, a crime, and a race against time."

Xander rolled his eyes. "Are you into that too? My parents love it."

"What are you all talking about?" Wally asked.

"The Willowcroft Mystery Theater Show on WoW—Waves of Willowcroft," Mrs. T explained. "It's well done. You should listen in."

Olivia's mouth dropped open. She grabbed Tammy's arm with a grip that made Tammy wince. "Didn't I see something in this week's Gazette about the Croft Comedy Jam having a teen show?"

"Yeah. I couldn't think of anything worse. No way I'm—" Xander began.

Olivia flashed a mischievous grin. "Come on, it'll be fun!"

Xander wagged a finger. "—not a chance. Don't even think it."

"But everyone who submits a comedy routine gets to tour the recording studio," Olivia said, batting her eyelids at him.

Brilliant. We can visit the bank and the studio to explore all three rooms.

"Aha," said Wally. "You'd be going undercover, Xander."

"Uh-uh. Not happening." He closed his laptop and hugged it to his chest like a shield.

Poor kid. People aren't his strong point, let alone being live on radio. But we need this.

"I'd jump at the chance to go undercover." Olivia put on an exaggerated pout. "But I'm too old to play a teenager." Her posture straightened, and her face became animated. "I'll help you write your routine and practice."

"It might be worse, dear," offered Mrs. T.

Xander shot Mrs. T a glare of horror.

"It's not like you're facing a live audience. It will just be you with a microphone and the host," Mrs. T encouraged. "The experience will do you the world of good. Increase your confidence."

"Who's the funniest person you know?" Olivia asked.

"I don't know any funny people," Xander replied, panic spreading across his face as he looked around for help.

"Of course you do, silly."

"Who?"

"ME!"

Xander gave a sideways glance, his face pleading for rescue, but the rest of the team were enjoying the exchange too much to intervene.

This is better than reality TV. And it might help solve the mystery.

Chapter 3

Monday morning at the Willowcroft Bank was quiet, making it the perfect time for their reconnaissance mission. The marble floors gleamed under the restored glass dome, and the original bronze teller cages gave the place an air of old-world sophistication.

Mrs. Hazel Temperance swept through the ornate doors, the peacock blue of her shawl trailing behind her like a royal banner. It was perfect for today's little adventure—the bold pattern conveyed confidence, and the wide fabric concealed a multitude of sins, or in this case, a cleverly packed handbag. Wally followed, his footsteps inaudible compared to the deliberate click of her sensible heels against the stone.

"Sheriff Wallace!" Owen, one of the security guards, straightened. "And Mrs. Temperance, always a pleasure." Owen was one of many in town who still referred to Wally as Sheriff. *We can use that.*

"Owen, dear," Hazel went into dramatic mode, bringing out the precise British lilt she'd inherited from her mother, perfect for projection across a classroom of restless teenagers—or a bank lobby. "I simply must access my safety deposit box. The most urgent matter, you understand."

At the counter, a female teller beamed. "Of course, Mrs. Temperance! And how's the knitting circle? Mom said your lemon drizzle cake last week was divine."

"Well, if it isn't Beatrice Smith's daughter. The cake is all in the timing, dear. Speaking of timing..." She glanced at her wristwatch. "I do hope this won't take long. I have a rather pressing engagement at eleven." A lie, but necessary for the mission.

"I'll escort you down," Owen offered.

Wally stepped forward, badge-less but still commanding respect. "I need to verify some old records. Part of a cold case review. Mind if I tag along?"

Owen's eyes lit up. "A cold case, Sheriff? Like in those true crime shows?"

"Something similar," Wally said.

They descended the stairs to the vault level. The temperature dropped several degrees, raising goosebumps on Hazel's arms beneath her blouse. She chatted about her urgent need to retrieve her grandmother's brooch for an imaginary photoshoot while peppering Owen with questions about his mother's arthritis.

"Poor Martha. Has she tried the lavender balm I suggested? It works wonders on my creaky knees in wintertime."

The vault door stood open during business hours, its massive steel frame a testament to the bank's security—at this entrance, anyway. Owen led them past the cash room into the first safety deposit room where Hazel's box was located.

"I'll need to check some measurements in the other room too," Wally mentioned. "For the case file."

Mrs. Temperance let out a theatrical gasp. "Oh fudgsicle!" She clutched her shawl. "Is that... a spider?"

Owen's head whipped around. "Where?"

"There! By the corner!" She waved her arm with dramatic emphasis while her purse tumbled from her grasp, scattering its contents across the floor. "Oh dear, oh dear!"

As Owen bent to help gather her strewn belongings—an impressive array of knitting needles, hard candies, and a ball of yarn that rolled under a cabinet with perfect timing—Wally slipped into the second room.

Hazel fumbled with her things, knocking over more items as Owen reached for the runaway yarn. Harold would have laughed himself silly seeing his proper wife creating such chaos in a bank vault.

"Sheriff?" Owen called out. "Everything okay in there?"

"Just measuring," Wally called back.

Hazel pressed a hand to her chest. "Owen, dear, would you be an absolute angel and fetch me a glass of water? All this excitement..."

"Of course, Mrs. Temperance. Sheriff, would you...?"

"I'll stay with her," Wally said, stepping back into the first room. As soon as Owen's footsteps faded, they exchanged looks.

"Find anything?"

"The room *is* smaller than the blueprints suggest, and there's something behind the back wall that isn't concrete or dirt."

"Did you find any levers or latches?"

"Not enough time to check everything." He pulled out his dinging phone.

He turned the screen toward Mrs. Temperance. "Tammy sent this."

> **Tammy:** Found article about Prohibition tunnels under town. Maybe one leads to the bank?

She pointed to the back wall. "Could there be one right behind us?"

Owen's returning footsteps echoed in the hallway.

Hazel resumed her performance. "—and I said, 'That's not a tea cozy, dear, that's your cat!'" She accepted the water with a gracious smile.

Later, as they climbed the stairs, Owen asked, "Did you get everything you needed, Sheriff?"

"Might need to come back for a follow-up," Wally said.

Owen escorted them back upstairs and outside into the bright sunlight. The heat pressed against Hazel's skin after the cool interior of the bank.

"That was rather fun," she said. "Let's do it again sometime."

"You should have been an actress instead of a teacher."

"Oh, but I was both, dear. Where do you think I perfected my 'I saw a spider' routine? Thirty years of classroom management teaches one all sorts of useful deceptions. Not to mention I directed many school plays."

Wally glanced at the Sheriff's Department.

"I assume you'll be paying Sheriff Stanton a visit," said Hazel.

Wally nodded. "I might as well straight out ask for the case file."

"Didn't Beverly promise you the archive key anytime you wanted it after getting justice for Mary Collins?"

"I'll keep Bev as a back-up for when I really need it. It's not an open case anymore thanks to us. I'm sure Stanton will give it up. Are you heading to the bookstore?"

"No, I'm heading to Serenity Gardens. I want to ask Eleanor about the tunnels Tammy mentioned."

"Max Cross's sister?" Wally raised an eyebrow. "Good thinking."

"One never knows what people remember about their younger days."

Xander slumped in his chair in the back room of Bookworm Haven, his laptop balanced on his knees. The murder board loomed behind him, covered in photos of the bank blueprints they'd pieced together yesterday.

His code editor was open, a half-written program designed to map the town's old tunnel system if he could concentrate long enough to finish it. But Olivia's excitement was making that impossible.

"Your parents think it's wonderful you're branching out socially with the comedy show." Olivia buzzed with enthusiasm as she cleared space on the table.

"That explains the weirdness this morning when I said I was heading to the bookstore." *Wait. What?* His stomach dropped. "You've talked to my parents about it?"

"A quick chat over coffee to get their consent at the diner this morning. But that's not important right now." She waved a hand. "What matters is that in just over a week, you'll be performing your comedy routine at the Croft Comedy Jam, and—" she did jazz hands "—we get a backstage tour of the recording studio!"

His laptop teetered on his knees. "But I don't have a routine. I don't know how to be funny!"

"That's why you have me!" Olivia pulled out a notebook covered in what looked like random words connected by arrows. "I was brainstorming all night. I was voted 'Most Likely to Host SNL' in college."

"Really?"

"Well, no. But I would've been if it had been a category." She adjusted her glasses, grinning. "Now, what makes you laugh?"

Xander's mind went blank. What did make him laugh? Coding jokes? But normal people didn't find those funny. "Uh... cat videos?"

"Perfect! We can work with that. Watch this—" Olivia stood up, assuming what she probably thought was a commanding stance. "Why did the cat get kicked off the computer? Because she kept showing her mouse pad!"

The silence was deafening.

"Get it? Mouse pad? Like a computer mouse?" She wiggled her eyebrows.

Xander wished his hair was long enough to hide behind. "Let's try something else?"

"Ooh, you're right. Too obvious. How about this one: What did the HTML coding cat say? Tag, you're it!"

His fingers hovered over the keyboard, shielding it from digital embarrassment. "Olivia, I don't think—"

"No, no, you're right again. Too niche. We need something broader. What about..." She consulted her notebook. "Oh! Why did the programmer quit his job? Because he didn't get arrays!"

"That's..." Xander searched for a diplomatic response. "One of kind of—"

"Terrible." Tammy's voice came as she walked through the disguised bookshelf doorway. "Sorry, Olivia, but stick to genealogy."

"Everyone's a critic," Olivia huffed, but her eyes still sparkled. "Fine, what would you suggest?"

Xander's phone buzzed. A message from his dad: "Proud of you for trying something new, kiddo. Break a leg!"

Great. It was too late to back out.

"What if," he said, an idea forming, "I did something about what it's like being a teenager in a small town? You know, like how everyone knows your business before you do?" *Like how your parents can approve your entry into a comedy competition without telling you first.*

Olivia's face lit up. "Yes! And about how your dad's the park ranger, so everyone expects you to be this outdoorsy person..."

"But instead I'm inside writing code to track the town's weather patterns," Xander said. *That might work.*

"Now that's funny," Tammy said. "Because it's real."

Olivia flopped into her chair, pouting. "I still think my jokes had potential."

"No," Xander and Tammy said in unison.

As Xander opened a new document to write his routine, he realized something. Whether the routine was good or bad didn't matter. What mattered was getting into the radio station. And if making a fool of himself helped solve the mystery of Max Cross's stolen money, well... at least he'd have something funny to joke about later.

Mrs. T arrived at Serenity Gardens Nursing Home with a basket of fresh scones. Eleanor Bennett had a sweet tooth. The warm, buttery scent wafted through the disinfected-soaked hallway, drawing appreciative glances from the staff.

She found Eleanor, Max's sister, sitting in the common room, working on a crossword puzzle. Her wrinkled hands shook as she filled in the boxes. Her short, white hair framed a face etched with wisdom and a sense of release from the revelations she'd shared about her late brother.

"Good morning, Eleanor."

"Ah, Hazel," she spied the now-open basket. "I see you've brought scones... I assume you want some information about my brother?"

"You know me too well, dear." Hazel settled into the adjacent armchair, its cushion exhaling as it accepted her weight.

"And you know how to get an old lady talking." She snatched a scone and took a bite. Strawberry jam dribbled down her chin, a drop landing on her pale blue cardigan.

Hazel handed her a napkin from the basket. "I wanted to ask you about old Willowcroft. A newspaper article mentioned tunnels used during Prohibition. Do you recall anything about them?"

Eleanor froze mid-bite. She dabbed at her chin, her hands steadier than moments before, as if the mention of the tunnels had awakened something vital within her. "Those tunnels were quite the legend when I was a girl. All us kids dreamed of finding an entrance and exploring them. I begged Max to help me search."

"Did you find an entry point?" Hazel's fingers dug into the armrest.

Eleanor shook her head, slow and deliberate. "But the older folks in town told stories. They spoke of buildings having concealed entrances. Some said you could travel from one corner of the square to the other without seeing daylight. However, we were never able to confirm anything."

"Never mind," Hazel said, giving her hand a comforting squeeze.

Eleanor sighed. "I'd love to see those tunnels before I die, to satisfy my childhood curiosity." Her fingers tightened around Hazel's. "Whatever you're looking for, I hope you find it. And when you do... Promise you'll wheel me down there?"

Wally clutched the Sweet Crumbs pastry box against his chest as he pushed through the sheriff's office door.

"Morning, Stanton. Got a minute?" He flipped open the pastry box lid, revealing an array of sugary delights—his secret weapon of persuasion.

Stanton's eyes widened like a suspect caught in a lie. He licked his lips and patted his round belly. "For a bear claw? I've got five." His thick fingers snatched the largest pastry, and he bit into it with enthusiasm. Powdered sugar dusted his uniform. "What can I do for you?"

Wally maintained eye contact—a technique he'd perfected during countless interrogations. "I was hoping you'd share the case files from Max's heist."

Stanton froze mid-chew. He wiped sugar from his mouth with the back of his hand, leaving a white smear across his knuckles. "That investigation is closed... because of you, I might add."

Wally fixed him with the same stare that had broken hardened criminals in Boston.

Stanton's resistance crumbled. He sighed, shoulders slumping in defeat. "All right. Bev already told me she's giving you the archives key whenever you ask. I might as well hand over the file and keep tabs on what you're up to."

He plucked a worn folder from the "to be filed" tray and slid it across the desk. Crumbs scattered across the manila surface.

"I have to thank you and your team for helping us reveal Max Cross as the murderer and thief." Stanton's tone shifted from resignation to professional concern. "But be careful. When money is involved, people become unpredictable."

"Don't worry." Wally tucked the file under his arm. "We'll be cautious. We want to solve the puzzle of *how* Max did it. I appreciate the help."

He typed a quick text to Olivia and stepped out into the square, heading toward Bookworm Haven. He'd promised to man the store while she and Xander went undercover at the radio station.

Time to analyze the facts.

Chapter 4

Xander's grin evaporated faster than an unsaved file. "Now? But Wally's got the file—"

"It will be here when we get back," Olivia said, already gathering her things. "The tour starts in twenty minutes."

His stomach did that familiar flip it always did before public speaking. Or any speaking. "Can we reschedule? I mean, the radio station isn't going anywhere..."

"We need to examine the wall," Olivia said.

Wally arrived as Xander considered faking a computer emergency. The retired sheriff took one look at Xander's face and chuckled. "Stage fright?"

"More like examining-a-crime-scene fright," Xander mumbled.

"You'll be fine," Olivia assured him, handing Wally her spare set of keys. "Think of it as hacking, but in person."

The walk to the radio station took forever, or maybe three minutes—Xander couldn't tell anymore. The summer heat wasn't helping his nerves, making his palms sweaty against his laptop case. He'd insisted on bringing it, claiming he might need to reference his routine, but really, having it in his hands kept the panic at bay.

The station's entrance was the bank's old side door, now sporting a neon "WoW" sign and a poster advertising the teen comedy competition. Inside, the modern reception area clashed with the building's historic architecture, as if the building had downloaded a software update and only half of it had installed.

"Olivia Huddlestone and Xander Simmons for the tour," Olivia announced to the receptionist, whose expression mirrored a Windows update for enthusiasm.

"Down the stairs, second door. DJ Rick is expecting you."

A man entered the door ahead of them. "Greg Wescott," said Olivia. "From the morning show."

Who?

The space opened up to multiple desks and people milling around.

DJ Rick turned out to be a middle-aged man wearing a Hawaiian shirt and dad jeans, with the kind of enthusiasm that made Xander want to crawl into his laptop and hide in the code.

"Welcome to the home of Waves of Willowcroft!" Rick's voice had a radio-perfect quality even off-air. "Let's start with our state-of-the-art recording studio."

As they followed Rick along the corridor, Olivia appraised everything they passed. "The acoustics must be amazing with these thick walls," she said, trailing her hand along the surface. "Almost like a vault of sound."

Xander rolled his eyes.

"This used to be part of the old bank vault!" Rick beamed. "We added extra soundproofing, of course, but these walls are as solid as they come."

The studio itself was smaller than Xander expected, though his tech-brain cataloged the impressive array of equipment. But Olivia was more interested in the walls, moving around the room like she was checking out ingredients at Mrs. Hubbard's Cupboard.

"Mind if I... absorb the atmosphere?" she asked, pressing her hands against the back wall. "I find it helps with creative energy."

Rick gave a bemused shrug. "Take your time. Most kids want to play with the sound effects."

Olivia "absorbed the atmosphere" of every inch of the back wall, while Xander pretended to be fascinated by the mixing board. He really wanted to find a way to scan for hollow spaces behind the walls. But Rick ushered them toward the broadcast booth.

"This is where the magic happens," Rick announced, not noticing Olivia's disappointed glance back at the recording studio. "Now, who wants to try their hand at being a DJ?"

Xander caught Olivia's eye. She shook her head. She'd found nothing. Too many changes with the extra soundproofing. *One chance blown already.*

As Rick demonstrated the complex array of buttons and sliders on the broadcast console, Xander's attention split between the equipment and Olivia's increasingly desperate signals. *She's terrible at subtle.* Her head tilts toward the recording studio grew more exaggerated, adding frantic hand gestures that could have been charades for "create a diversion" or "I'm choking on air."

What am I supposed to do? I can't just knock something over—this equipment costs more than my college fund. His palms dampened. *Think, think!*

"DJ Rick," Xander said, pulling out his laptop with hands he forced not to tremble. "I noticed something interesting about your audio setup. Mind if I show you?"

"You know about sound systems?"

"A little." *More than you, probably, but that sounds arrogant.* Xander opened his laptop, positioning it so Rick would have to turn his back to the door. "I've been working on some programs for audio processing." He opened a spectrograph program he'd been developing. "Would you mind checking this out? I'd love a professional opinion."

Please buy this. Please, please buy this.

"Well, well!" Rick leaned in. "This is pretty sophisticated stuff for someone your age."

For someone my age. Always with the qualifiers. From the corner of his eye, Xander saw Olivia slip out. *Perfect. At least I didn't screw this part up.*

"See, I'm trying to optimize the frequency response curve," Xander explained, launching into dense technical details. *He's not following any of this. Good. Keep talking. For once, being a tech nerd is useful.*

Rick's eyes glazed over, but he nodded along. *Dad wouldn't recognize me right now. Leading a conversation? Creating a diversion? Who even am I?*

Xander's confidence wavered. *She's taking too long. What if someone catches her? What if I run out of tech babble?* His heart raced as he improvised. "The real problem appears in the tertiary harmonics stage..."

Where IS she?

"...which might explain the interference patterns in the lower frequencies," Xander continued, voice steady despite the panic building inside him. *If she gets caught, it's on me. All on me.*

Olivia reappeared, her cheeks flushed but appearing satisfied.

Finally. "...and that's what I think might be the problem," Xander finished, relief flooding through him. He wasn't useless with people after all.

"Fascinating stuff," Rick said. Xander resisted the urge to ask which ten percent he understood. "We might have an internship opening this fall if you're interested..."

Xander was proud that his technical knowledge had provided cover for Olivia's extracurricular activities. If only tech talk worked in all social situations. Surely he no longer needed to perform in the comedy competition with their mission over.

Outside, Olivia bounced with excitement. "That was brilliant, Xander! Though I have to say, watching Rick try to follow your explanation was almost as entertaining as your comedy routine."

"Did you find anything?"

She grinned. "I may have dropped my earring and had to feel around the baseboards to find it. Multiple times."

"The old dropped earring trick?"

"Classic detective work never fails." She patted his shoulder. "And you, my young friend, are turning into quite the undercover agent yourself."

"But did you find anything?"

Olivia's smile dropped. "The padding made it impossible to tell anything about the original walls." She sighed. "How ridiculous was I, pressing my ear against every surface like I was trying to hear the ocean in a seashell?"

"At least we tried," Xander offered. "And hey, we know the layout now. Something in the case file might make more sense after seeing the space."

Olivia perked up. "True. Technical talk did the trick. Your parents were right—you're flourishing with this detective work."

Heat crept up Xander's neck, but for once, it wasn't from embarrassment. He might not be good at telling jokes or making small talk, but give him a computing problem to solve? That was his element. He'd learned the technical jargon trick when he had to convince Stanton he hadn't hacked the school records during the Great Bear Caper—when, of course, he had.

"Now," Olivia said as they headed back to the bookstore, "let's see what Wally found out. This mystery's turning into a recipe with half the ingredients missing."

"Maybe we're looking in the wrong places."

Tammy sat forward as everyone returned from their excursions, eager to hear what they'd uncovered. She waited for her turn while Wally paced the floor.

"No witnesses at all in the case file," he said. "And, as with the murder, forensics wasn't a thing then. No DNA analysis or ear prints."

"Ear prints?" Xander echoed, intrigued by the concept.

"Yup," Wally replied. "Criminals sometimes leave ear prints behind when they press their ears against doors or windows to listen for sounds inside. It's not as common as fingerprints, but it has been used to catch criminals before."

"I don't believe you." Xander searched on his phone. "It says ear print evidence started being used in 1965. It's real. But too late for us."

Tammy clutched her phone and seized the opportunity to share her finds. "So, Lockie and I found something interesting." She cleared her throat, tapping her phone screen to wake it up. "Most of what we dug up was more typical small-town fare—pie contests, fundraisers. But then we stumbled onto this."

She presented her phone. The 1926 photograph offered a glimpse into Willowcroft's shadowy past. "Deputies raiding a speakeasy here in Willowcroft. The caption mentions underground tunnels used for bootlegging."

Mother would call this a wild goose chase. But you don't belong here anymore, Mother.

Her friends' eyes widened.

"The tunnels could explain how Max got in and out unseen," Olivia said.

Tammy swiped through the old black-and-white photos she had surreptitiously snapped at the library. "I found a bunch of photos from the 1920s and 1930s, but they wouldn't let me make copies," Tammy explained.

"There might be some clues in here." Her writer's mind itched to spin the grainy images into stories, but she forced herself to focus on the facts.

Everyone gathered around her, their shoulders pressing in.

Lockie jumped onto the table, his tail swishing as he peered at the phone. *At least he didn't get us permanently banned from the library.* Tammy remembered Maxine's glacial glare at Lockie's antics.

"I have a projector at home," said Xander. "We can use it to enlarge the photos. I'll bring it in tomorrow."

Mrs. Temperance clapped her hands. "Excellent idea. We'll be able to see so much more when the images are larger."

"Someone refresh my memory about Prohibition," Olivia said.

Mrs. T straightened in her chair, but Xander jumped in faster. "Prohibition started in 1920 with the passage of the 18th Amendment. It banned the production, transportation, and sale of intoxicating liquors."

"Intoxicating liquors? Sounds like something my grandpa would say," said Wally.

"Actually, dear," said Mrs. T, "Michigan banned it three years earlier in 1917, with some individual towns being dry as far back as 1907. The law was supposed to stop the consumption of alcohol, but it created an enormous market for bootleg booze."

Trying to control one thing only creates a bigger problem somewhere else.

"The ban lasted until 1933 when it was repealed by the 21st Amendment," continued Mrs. T. "But during that time, an entire underground world sprang up."

Xander turned his laptop around to show the group a grainy old photograph of men loading wooden crates into a truck by moonlight.

"They had to get creative with sneaking the alcohol around," he said. "They used underground tunnels to store and transport the illegal stash right here in our town and many others, being so close to Canada where the rules were different."

Xander scanned his notes. "From what I can tell, the Willowcroft tunnel system stretched all over, connecting secret basements of homes and businesses that were fronts for bootleggers and speakeasies."

"Wow," Tammy breathed, her imagination igniting. Hidden passages, concealed rooms, clandestine meetings—this town was a gold mine of story material.

My old literary agent would have told me to milk it for all it's worth.

"The tunnels could have been the perfect escape route for Max Cross after the heist," said Mrs. Temperance.

"Exactly," Xander agreed, showing them more photos. "Like Tammy's, these will benefit from being enlarged tomorrow."

Mrs. T added, "Eleanor said they never found the tunnels as kids. Max forgot to tell his sister."

Or deliberately kept it to himself.

"We're one step closer to finding the truth," said Olivia.

"Finding those tunnels is the key to tracking Max's escape route," said Mrs. T.

Wally rubbed his hands together. "And we might find the lost loot there!"

Tammy gave him a look. "Let's not get ahead of ourselves. We need to find the tunnel entrance first." *One plot point at a time, or the whole story falls apart.*

Xander closed his laptop with a snap. "Agreed. I'm sure we'll find clues in the photos."

Olivia stretched and stifled a yawn. "I'm beat. I say we call it a night and regroup in the morning."

Murmurs of assent rippled through the group as they gathered their things. Tammy scooped up Lockie, his sleepy purr vibrating through her fingers.

"Bright and early tomorrow, then!"

Chapter 5

Tammy always got a thrill from pushing the disguised door into their secret lair. She and Lockie were the last to arrive in the back room. Lockie bolted to the bags thrown in the corner for a sniff.

"Do you have everything you need for the projector?" Olivia asked.

Xander hoisted his equipment bag. "All set."

Wally clapped. "Let's get this show on the road."

The makeshift screen flickered to life with the uploaded photos under Xander's rapid setup. Tammy settled into a chair.

For the next few hours, they worked through the historical photographs Tammy and Xander had found. Tammy's coffee grew cold beside her as they analyzed newspaper clippings and faded pictures.

By late morning, they'd built a timeline on the backside of the whiteboard connecting events in Willowcroft during Prohibition with colored yarn from Mrs. T's knitting bag and pushpins.

"This is the last one," said Xander.

A grainy black-and-white image expanded across the wall. A storefront materialized, the sign "Willowcroft Apothecary" now crystal clear where it had been unreadable at the library.

"This is the speakeasy bust from the twenties." Tammy found the accompanying article. "This photo was taken after police caught bootleggers operating from a tunnel beneath the building."

Wally approached the screen, his nose inches from the projection. "Is this the Swinging Spoon? Same roofline, same window arrangement."

"You're right!" Mrs. T exclaimed, checking her watch. "It's almost noon. Lunch at the Swinging Spoon to scope out the place?"

"Fieldwork," said Olivia, grabbing her keys. "Tuesday's slow anyway. I'll close the store. Let's find those tunnels."

"Wait." Wally backed toward the door. "Give me twenty to grab my gear in case we find something."

"Same here." Mrs. T followed him. "Knitting circle this afternoon, but I'll grab an apple pie from Sweet Crumbs on the way. Marjorie and Betty have keys if I'm late."

"Let's meet in front of the Swinging Spoon at twelve-thirty," Olivia said. "That gives everyone time to get what they need."

At twelve-thirty sharp, Tammy and the team gathered on the sidewalk outside the diner, comparing their preparations.

"Light sources for everyone." Wally unzipped his backpack, revealing flashlights.

"Navigation covered." Xander displayed his phone with the offline GPS tracker app and held up an old-school compass.

Mrs. T grinned as she extracted a faded bike helmet from her oversized purse. "Protection for my old head, just in case."

Olivia distributed whistles. "I use these when I go solo hiking, but they'll help us find each other if we get separated." She blew a quick toot.

"Good thinking, everyone," Tammy said, watching Lockie, who blinked sleepily after his power nap. "I brought our feline friend here. He's got a knack for sniffing out clues, and he has a red light on his collar."

"Speaking of sniffing things out," Wally said, "I'm starving. Let's get inside."

Grilling meat assaulted Tammy's sinuses as they claimed a booth with clear sightlines to the kitchen.

"So there's potentially a tunnel entrance somewhere in this building." Tammy kept her voice low, conscious of eavesdroppers. In her books, the villain always lurked nearby, collecting intel. "We need to find a discreet way to check out the back areas."

"Let's divide and conquer," Olivia suggested. "Some of us can chat with the staff while others keep an eye out."

"Solid approach." Mrs. T nodded. "And let's not forget about Lockie; he might lead us straight to it."

Under the table, Lockie's tail swished against Tammy's ankle. Even he sensed they were close.

"Operation Tunnel starts after lunch." Wally stuffed the last bite of his burger into his mouth. "Remember, we're searching for any signs of a disguised entrance or anything else connected to those tunnels."

"Let's just ask." Xander raised his hand, flagging down Peggy, the owner.

"Direct approach. Smart." Tammy manufactured her friendliest smile as Peggy approached. "Hey Peggy, we're researching Willowcroft's Prohibition history. Any chance we could check out your basement? We think there may have been a speakeasy there in the twenties."

Peggy hesitated, glancing between the team members.

Say yes, say yes.

Peggy tilted her head. "I don't see why not. It's nothing but a boring storage room." She tapped her order pad. "But don't disturb my staff. Gardener's Club discount day has us swamped."

"Perfect!" Olivia said. "We promise to be respectful."

When Peggy retreated, Wally hunched forward. "Time to establish roles. I'll scan for any structural anomalies that could indicate a passage."

"I'll see if I can glean any psychic impressions from the space," Mrs. T added, earning surprised looks from the table.

Xander patted his pocket. "Photo documentation."

"Written records." Olivia brandished her notebook.

"Lockie and I will follow his instincts." Tammy scratched behind his ears.

Lockie rumbled a purr, focused as if he understood the assignment.

"We'll leave no stone unturned, and I mean we are lifting every stone we find," Xander said.

The clatter of plates and hum of conversation surrounded them. Tammy soaked in the small-town ambiance—so different from her former city life, yet infinitely more inspiring for her writing.

Peggy returned, wiping her hands on her apron. "Ready for a basement tour?"

They slipped into a narrow hallway past the kitchen. A door marked *Employees Only* yielded to Peggy's key. Wooden stairs descended into darkness.

"Check it out all you want, but stay out of my staff's way." Peggy flipped a switch, igniting a single bare bulb.

"Won't be a bother." Wally accepted the responsibility.

"Stay sharp, everyone." Tammy's mouth dried with anticipation. This was straight out of chapter twelve in her first thriller.

Wally distributed flashlights. "Let's move."

Xander activated his GPS tracker. "Signal's weak."

"That's why we have these." Olivia clutched her whistle.

Mrs. T secured her helmet straps.

The stairs creaked under their weight. At the bottom was a dingy room crowded with shelves and mystery-filled boxes. Tammy coughed as their footsteps kicked up puffs of dirt from the concrete floor. She peered into the gloomy corners, heart pounding.

Tammy directed her beam across crumbling brick walls and metal shelving units. Musty air pressed against her face. A faded sign declaring "Storage - Keep Out!" hung crookedly over one section.

"This is promising," she said, moving closer to examine the bricks.

"Any ideas on what we should do?" Xander panned his light across the ceiling.

"I'll search behind these crates." Wally approached a stack of wooden boxes with faded lettering. "Perfect hiding spot."

The others spread out through the room, each scanning a different section of the basement. Tammy tracked Lockie's movements as he prowled between boxes, his nose working overtime.

"Just kitchen junk back here." Wally's voice echoed from behind a shelf. He emerged holding a dusty bottle. "Old whiskey, though."

Xander examined the label. "I bet that's from the bootlegging days. We're on the right track."

Olivia rapped the walls with her knuckles. "Hmm, some of these sound hollow. But honestly, I wouldn't have a clue what hollow sounds like. But I wonder..."

"Brick doesn't work for the sound test," Wally said.

Olivia shrugged, as if it was good enough and kept knocking.

Lockie's ears pricked. He scampered to the far corner and rose on his hind legs, pawing at the wall.

"Lockie's onto something!" Tammy rushed over. Her fingers traced the brick where Lockie scratched.

One brick wiggled.

Not a brick.

She pulled, revealing a disguised handle.

The camouflaged door—painted to match the surrounding wall—featured a faintly etched cocktail glass. Tammy tugged. The door swung open with a groan, releasing a rush of stale, damp air making her eyes water.

"Secret tunnel confirmed!"

"The knocking test would have discovered that," said Olivia.

Wally aimed his beam into the opening. Tammy covered her nose against the dank odor. Stone steps vanished into blackness.

Mrs. T squeezed Tammy's shoulder. "Now the real adventure begins!"

Like Midnight's Last Secret *except this is real.* She looked at the others. *These friends are real.* And whatever waited in that darkness was real too.

"Max's lost bank loot, here we come!" Olivia stared into the void.

"Stay close," Wally warned, switching on his headlamp.

They entered the passageway one by one, flashlights creating overlapping pools of light.

"Check this out." Xander pointed to a carved pestle-and-mortar symbol on the tunnel side of the door. "This marks the entrance to the apothecary, which was here before the Swinging Spoon, to help find your way out."

"Prohibition forced people to get creative," Mrs. T said.

"Unbelievable," Wally whispered. "Never thought I'd find something like this beneath our feet."

"How much did these passageways have to do with Max Cross's bank robbery and Mary Collins's murder?" Olivia's question hung in the air.

Tammy stepped deeper into the darkness. "Only one way to find out."

Chapter 6

Darkness swallowed them whole. Tammy swept her flashlight along the tunnel walls, revealing damp brick lined with cobwebs and decades of grime. Mold and musty earth filled her nostrils with each cautious breath. Ahead, Lockie's blinking red collar bobbed like a tiny beacon, guiding their descent.

Olivia charged ahead without hesitation, her footsteps confident on the stone steps. Tammy envied her fearlessness, the way her friend barreled into the unknown as if danger were merely an inconvenience rather than something to dread.

Tammy pictured the apothecary owner sneaking down here during Prohibition, bottles clinking as he transported his illicit cargo to thirsty customers.

A cobweb brushed against her cheek. She shuddered, a wave of revulsion prickling her skin, hoping the web hadn't left anything behind. She swiped at her face, suppressing a yelp. *Get it together. You've written scarier scenes than this.*

Water dripped somewhere ahead. Or was it behind? The irregular patter seemed to come from multiple directions, disorienting her. The stench of stale alcohol lingered, making her wrinkle her nose.

Their beams caught something glinting in the darkness.

"Look." She directed her light at glass bottles emerging from the shadows, their dirty surfaces reflecting emerald and amber hues. Beside them sat rickety wooden crates with aged, warped slats, but still intact.

"These are..." She knelt, her trembling fingers hovering above a bottle's neck, nervous to touch something so well preserved from another era. She swallowed hard. "Prohibition artifacts. Untouched for a century."

Rising, Tammy moved along the path, sweeping the darkness ahead. Wine barrels lined the walls. *I can't help myself.* She pressed her palm against the rough, splintered wood. The physical connection to the past ignited her writer's soul.

"Wow," Xander breathed, stepping closer to examine an unopened bottle.

"Imagine the stories these walls could tell," Tammy said. Lockie meowed, as if agreeing with her assessment. She began drafting a scene with a nervous bootlegger, footsteps overhead, and the desperate need to remain silent.

"Indeed," Mrs. Temperance said. "This discovery is truly extraordinary. We should document everything we find."

"Already am, Mrs. T," Xander replied. "If I see everything through the screen, it's not as scary."

Xander hunched behind his camera, his shoulders tense, body angled toward the exit. While his fingers moved with confident precision across his device, his eyes darted between the screen and the darkness beyond. He used his camera as a shield, like she sometimes used her notebook. Easier to face the world through a lens than head on.

Tammy leaned over a barrel, directing her flashlight into its depths. Brackish liquid pooled at the bottom. Her breath created ripples.

"These barrels must be over a hundred years old." She inhaled the musty-sweet smell emanating from the disturbed liquid. The scent transported her to a bygone era. Her fingers tingled with the urgent need to transform this sensory experience into words on a page.

"Can you believe we're walking through history?" Olivia asked.

"The people who used these tunnels were breaking the law," Wally said, "risking everything for a taste of something forbidden."

"Some people will do anything for what they want," Mrs. T said.

"A fact I've learned too well over the years," Wally added.

"Anything for money, you mean," Tammy said.

The brick walls told their own silent story. Expert craftsmanship, built to last—and stay concealed. Tammy trailed her fingers along the cool surface, appreciating the care taken by those who had constructed this underground network.

"Think about it," she said. "If Max Cross used these tunnels to escape after the bank robbery, he must have known about them long before. He could have spent years planning, studying every twist and turn."

"But why would he involve himself in something so risky? What drove him to steal and kill?" Olivia asked.

"Desperation," Mrs. Temperance suggested.

"Or greed. Or both," Wally added. "People are capable of terrible things when pushed to their limits."

"I don't care about his reasons," Xander said. "I want to find the money."

He opened a wooden crate. Dust billowed out, triggering a coughing fit. Inside sat rows of exotic glass bottles, some still sealed with wax. "I think this says 'Scotch Whiskey, 1912.'"

Wally whistled. "That bottle's worth a fortune now."

Tammy grinned. The scene unfolded in her mind: midnight deliveries, hushed voices, the clink of bottles, and the fear of discovery. This place was a novelist's goldmine.

Olivia illuminated a narrow opening branching from the main tunnel. "Let's see where this goes. To the treasure chamber we go."

Lockie trotted onward, leading their expedition deeper into the earth. Their beams crisscrossed, highlighting more relics as they delved beneath the town.

Lockie's collar flashed red as he paused. Tammy tensed, muscles tightening. She raised her hand, signaling the others to stop. *Has Lockie found something?*

She held her breath, straining to hear. A soft, rhythmic sound echoed along the passage. Thump-thump...thump-thump. The unmistakable bass notes of a piano rolled out of the darkness.

"It's got to be coming from the surface," Olivia said.

Wally checked his phone. "No signal."

"Let's follow the music," Xander suggested. "Maybe we can figure out where it's coming from."

They pressed on. The piano music grew louder, clearer, then stopped.

Tammy halted at a fork in the tunnel. *Left or right?* The choice loomed before her like a plot decision. Choose wrong, and the story falls flat.

"Which way do we go?" Xander asked.

As if responding, a faint melody started from the right passage. The haunting tune in a minor key raised goosebumps on Tammy's arms.

"There's our answer," she said, her throat dry.

They followed the right tunnel, a straight passage sloping downward. Her ears strained to follow the eerie music pulling them forward like an invisible thread.

Olivia grabbed her arm. "Look!"

Light filtered from above. *But how?* The piano notes rang clearer, each keystroke vibrant and precise.

Tammy held her breath as they reached the source. Wally boosted Xander for a better look.

"It's a basement grate," he whispered, excitement coloring his voice. "I see shelves of music books. We're under the Robinsons' place!"

"The piano teacher!" Mrs. T exclaimed. "Her house is a block behind the bank."

A network beneath the entire town. Passages connecting everything.

They continued onward, leaving the piano music behind. The air grew colder against her skin. *How far do these go?*

"Come on," Olivia urged. "The bank entrance has to be close, or back the other way."

Lockie padded ahead, his red collar flashing in rhythmic pulses.

"Yowl!"

Tammy jumped. *What now?*

Lockie stood rigid, fur bristling as he stared into a dark recess. Tammy rushed over. A strangled sound caught in her throat. "Over here."

The team huddled around her. Wally knelt, examining something half-buried in dirt. Their combined beams spotlighted a jumble of human bones.

"Is that... a skeleton?" Mrs. T asked, an audible gulp following.

"I'm afraid so," Wally confirmed. "I don't like this. Stay back."

"I'm not making the knitting circle, am I?" Mrs. T asked.

Olivia pushed past Xander. "Let me see!" she insisted, jumping to peek over him. "I'm not squeamish like some people."

Xander backed away, his face blanching. "Skeletons aren't my thing, even if it would be useful for biology class."

Tammy studied the remains, her pulse hammering in her ears. The ultimate research opportunity—macabre, yet fascinating. "Another of Max's victims?" *A rival? A betrayer? A loose end he needed to tie up?* The possibilities multiplied.

"What a horrible way to die, alone in the dark," Olivia said.

"All right," Wally said, "we need to explore as much of these tunnels as we can before reporting this body. Once the sheriff is involved, it will be roped off as a crime scene."

"Agreed," Olivia said. "We owe it to whoever this poor soul is to find out what happened, but it can wait a few more minutes."

Tammy nodded. "Let's document everything so we have as much to go on as possible."

"Xander, snap away," Mrs. T instructed.

"Can I do it without looking?" Xander asked, his hands trembling.

"I'll do the bones," Wally said. "You do a wide perimeter." He took out his phone and photographed the scene from multiple angles.

They continued through the tunnel to a junction that split into three passages. They chose the widest one, following it until it branched again.

"This is getting complicated," Tammy said, noting how the temperature dropped the deeper they went. Her watch showed they'd been underground for a couple of hours now.

At the third junction, Tammy's flashlight caught a glint of glass—another stash of bottles, but also something else. She knelt beside them.

"Look at this." She directed her beam to an old poker table. Her fingertips hovered above the rotted baize, imagining the forbidden games once played here, the hushed voices, the clink of illicit liquor glasses, the rustle of money changing hands. Each sense memory filled her writer's notebook in her mind.

The table's legs had collapsed on one side, as if time itself had grown weary of holding up the past. "Can you imagine the stories this table could tell?"

The camera's flash blinded her as Xander captured the scene. "Got it," he said, his voice steadier now than when they'd discovered the bones.

"I'm losing track of where we've been," Wally admitted, arriving at yet another branch.

They paused for water, checking their phone batteries. Signals had disappeared long ago.

The maze of passages seemed endless, branching in all directions. They'd passed several collapses blocking their path. *What if one behind us collapses?*

"It's too big." Tammy stopped and sighed. "It'll take days, weeks, or more to explore everything. We'll have to come back another day."

Olivia checked her watch and exhaled. "We've been down here for hours. We should tell the sheriff about the body."

"Let's get out of here," Xander said.

Tammy bobbed her head from side to side. Part of her wanted to explore every inch of this underground world, to absorb its clandestine stories, but now was not the time.

"These tunnels could explain how Max escaped after the bank robbery," Wally said. "He had an entire underground network at his disposal. But the body takes precedence over a treasure hunt."

"True," Mrs. T sighed. "We should seek justice for the victim, like we did for Mary Collins. If the money is here, it's not going anywhere."

"Let's head back then," Xander said, turning around. "We've collected heaps of data we can analyze above ground."

They retraced their steps through the winding passages. The flashlights bathed patches of moldering walls and forgotten debris in light. *How many secrets are buried here? How many bodies?*

And why? The question nagged at her the most. *For money? Revenge? Or something more complex?* Max Cross was evolving from bank robber to potential serial killer. Her fictional villains seemed tame by comparison.

The damp chill penetrated deeper now. Tammy hugged her arms around herself. The writer in her was taking mental notes, storing away sensory details for future use. *A writer's mind finds inspiration even in the most disturbing circumstances.*

They located the door with the pestle and mortar marking and emerged into the Swinging Spoon's basement.

The diner's cheerful retro interior disoriented Tammy after the gloom below.

Peggy straightened from wiping the counter. "Have you been down there all this time? I thought you'd left without saying goodbye."

"Sorry, Peggy. We would never do that," Mrs. T apologized. "We made quite a discovery in your basement. There's a disguised door leading to a network of tunnels."

Peggy's eyes widened. "Tunnels? Under my diner?"

"And a body," Wally added.

Peggy gasped, her hand flying to her mouth. "A body? Lawdy be." She gripped the counter edge. A twist of guilt knotted in Tammy's stomach. They'd brought this chaos into Peggy's world.

"And here I've been serving pie and coffee right over a dead person?"

"We're so sorry," Olivia said. "You'll probably have to close while the sheriff investigates."

Peggy blew out a breath, her expression shifting from horror to resignation. "I understand. Terrible though, someone dying there."

Wally stepped forward. "We need to inform Stanton." He made the call.

"Yes, yes," Peggy said, meeting each of their gazes. "That person deserves a proper burial. Their family needs closure."

Xander shifted his weight from one foot to the other. "This could have something to do with Max Cross too. We think whoever it is might be…"

Peggy held up a hand. "Best leave the speculation to the sheriff. You did your part finding them." She smoothed her apron. "Now how about some pie while we wait for the sheriff?"

"Yes, please," Olivia and Xander said in unison as they settled at the counter.

Nothing like food to make everything better.

Peggy shuffled to the pie case. Her hands trembled as she cut cherry pie slices, the knife wobbling against the ceramic plate. Poor woman. Finding out you've been working above a body all these years would shake anyone to their core. She served each of them, then pulled up a stool beside Olivia.

"I know this won't be easy for you," Olivia said.

Peggy patted her hand, attempting a smile. "Well, if I have to close the store, at least I get to spend more time in my garden while the sun's shining."

Heavy boots struck the cobblestones outside.

Tammy exchanged glances with the others. *No turning back now.*

Peggy sighed and smoothed her apron once more. "I'd best put on a fresh pot of coffee for the boys."

"Where is it?" Stanton asked as he entered, deputies trailing behind him.

They led him to the basement door in silence. Tammy's pulse throbbed as the sheriff examined the hidden entrance.

"Well, I'll be."

The first flashlight beam cut through the darkness. Stanton let out a slow exhale.

"Marjorie Hubbard barged into my office earlier like a woman on a mission," he said as he descended. "Swore Mrs. Temperance had vanished from the knitting circle and 'foul play was afoot.' Said she had half a mind to interview suspects herself if I didn't hop to it." He shook his head.

"Figured it was a case of someone getting caught up in their crocheting and losing track of time. Didn't expect actual bones."

Tammy pressed her lips together, suppressing a laugh. *Mrs. Hubbard leading an investigation? I'd pay to see that.* She probably had a suspect list prepared before Stanton even grabbed his hat.

Tammy shivered, as the dank air reminded her of the situation they were in. She focused on navigating the uneven ground, each step careful and measured.

They wound through the passages. The sheriff grumbled about jurisdiction and securing the scene.

When they reached the bones, the sheriff crouched beside the remains, intense concentration etched on his face. He let out a low whistle. "What have you stumbled upon this time?"

Peggy had cleared them a booth by the window and brought coffee without asking. No one had touched it.

Outside, red and blue lights flashed against the glass, cutting across the syrup bottles like a warning. Deputies moved in and out, the kitchen door propped open as crime scene tape stretched across everything.

"They'll be down there awhile," Wally said, breaking the silence. "Stanton asked us to hang tight."

Tammy sat with her hands wrapped around the mug, more for warmth than comfort. The diner had never been this empty. Just them, Peggy, and the endless line of deputies and forensics techs.

Xander leaned forward, elbows on the table. "It's a murder board now."

Tammy looked up. "What?"

He turned to Olivia. "Back at the start, we talked about whether our board was still a murder board if we were solving a bank heist."

"And I said with our luck we'd find a body or two," said Tammy. "I was joking."

Mrs. Temperance's voice was quiet. "It's true now."

No one said it out loud, but the weight of it settled over them.

Olivia stirred her coffee but didn't drink. "We came here searching for a way into the bank vault."

"And find the loot," said Xander.

Wally nodded. "And now the sheriff's roping off the place."

Peggy passed by with a pot of coffee. "You folks all right?"

No one answered.

Tammy rubbed her arms, staring out at the blinking lights. "It's more than a bank heist. It's a death too."

Mrs. Temperance tugged her shawl tighter. "Well, stories shift. We'd better follow this one where it leads, like we did for Mary."

Can we solve an extra mystery?

Chapter 7

The following morning, after an exhausting evening of giving statements at the Sheriff's Department, Hazel strode into Serenity Gardens nursing home, disinfectant assaulting her nose. Her canary yellow shawl, a deliberate burst of cheer in this clinical place, swished around her.

The nursing home corridors never changed: same beige walls, same faint hum of fluorescent lights, same mixture of quiet despair and stubborn resilience. But today, Hazel carried news that might brighten these dreary halls, at least for one resident, making this an interesting visit.

"Good morning, Mrs. Temperance," Nurse Emma greeted her.

"Morning, dear." Hazel patted her gray bun, coaxing the stray hairs to be less obvious. "Off to see Mrs. Bennett."

"You know the way."

She did. Two lefts, one right, past the sunroom where three older ladies played cards with fierce concentration—though Hazel hardly considered herself one of them, even at seventy-five.

She rapped her knuckles against the wooden door. "Eleanor? It's Hazel Temperance."

"Come in, come in!" The voice sounded thin but eager.

Eleanor sat in her rocking chair by the window, hands folded in her lap like a schoolgirl awaiting instruction. Her frame had shrunk since the last visit, but her eyes held a lively spark.

"To what do I owe the pleasure of a visit again so soon?" Mrs. Bennett asked with a warm smile.

Hazel pulled up a chair. "I have some news for you."

Eleanor's brows rose. "No scones today?"

"I'm here to provide, not elicit, my dear." The phrase slipped out, one of her father's old sayings.

A click of Eleanor's tongue, playful and light. She leaned forward, hands gripping the rocker arms. "Well, don't keep me waiting."

"The tunnels..." Hazel began. "We've found them."

Eleanor gasped, a hand flying to her mouth. "They're real?"

"Yes! We found an entrance in the diner's basement." The excitement in her voice reminded Hazel of her classroom days, when she'd revealed some fascinating historical fact to wide-eyed students.

"I scarcely believe it." Eleanor's gaze drifted to the window, to the slice of Willowcroft visible beyond the glass. "The rumors were true! I spent hours searching for secret doors and passages, imagining all the adventures I'd have."

A faraway stare claimed Eleanor's face, transporting her to younger days. "The ultimate game of hide and seek those tunnels would have been. Max was always better at hiding—sly and sneaky, even then."

Eleanor chuckled. "To think, after all these years..." Her shoulders slumped. "But I'm too old now to explore them."

Hazel reached over and patted Eleanor's arm. Beneath her fingers, the skin was thin and fragile. "It's never too late for new discoveries, my friend. And though you can't join us, we'll share everything we find."

Hazel's fingers twisted around the fringe of her shawl. "There's something else. Something we found in those tunnels."

Eleanor's expression shifted, concern replacing excitement. "What is it?"

"We found human remains." Hazel kept her voice gentle but direct. "A skeleton."

Eleanor's hand trembled as she pressed it against her chest. "Oh my." Her breathing quickened. "Do they... know who it is?"

"Not yet. Sheriff Stanton is investigating." Hazel leaned forward, watching Eleanor's reaction. "It could be connected to Max and the bank robbery."

Eleanor's shoulders sagged. "Meaning my brother killed two people to cover up his actions." She shook her head.

"It's not a certainty," Hazel reminded her. "But I thought you should know."

Eleanor nodded, her lips pressed into a thin line. "Thank you for telling me. It's... difficult to hear, but necessary." She took a deep breath, steadying herself. "I want the whole truth."

"You're very brave," Hazel said, reaching for Eleanor's hand.

Eleanor straightened her shoulders, a glimmer of determination pushing past the lingering shock. *That's the ticket.* No use dwelling on limitations when there were still mysteries to solve.

"Speaking of secrets..." Eleanor hesitated, her frail hands fidgeting in her lap. "The janitor found something under my dresser." She glanced around the room, as if to ensure they were alone. "It belongs to my great-nephew."

She opened a drawer and extracted a worn journal. "I'm sure it's important."

Hazel's heart skipped. Nathan's notebook? Where he recorded his grandfather's dementia ramblings? This could change everything.

"May I?" Hazel extended her hand.

"Of course."

The notebook settled into her palm with a weight greater than that of paper and ink. Its pages might contain the missing pieces to the puzzle of Max Cross and the bank heist.

"I don't understand a word of it. My brother's mind was not well by the end," said Eleanor.

"But Nathan clearly saw something. Something that made him view you as a threat."

Hazel flipped through the pages. *Come on... tell me who the body is.*

"He must have dropped it that night," Eleanor continued, her voice quavering. "When he tried to..."

The sentence went unfinished. No need to speak aloud of what Nathan had tried to do. The image of Nathan standing over Eleanor with a pillow over her face was not something Hazel could forget. Thankfully, Tammy and she had stopped him in time.

Composing herself, Eleanor went on. "All those visits Nathan made to his grandfather, documenting every word." She shook her head. "He became so obsessed with the same greed that drove my brother that he now sits in a psychiatric ward for his trouble."

Hazel scanned the notebook. Words scattered in twos and threes across each page. Not a full sentence to be seen. Hieroglyphics might have been more comprehensible.

Closing the notebook, Hazel met Eleanor's anxious gaze head-on. "What's done is done." She held up the notebook. "This may hold the key to solving the rest of the mystery."

Relief flooded Eleanor's face. She grasped Hazel's hand with a firm grip. "Bless you and the rest of the team. Your dedication heartens me. Perhaps we can bring all of Max's wicked deeds to light."

"We will." Hazel meant it. Not for the satisfaction of solving a decades-old mystery, but for Eleanor's peace of mind.

She tucked the notebook into her handbag, her mind already racing. The words held little meaning on their own, but with Eleanor's added context, they became a promising lead.

"I must go," Hazel said, "but I'll be back with any progress we make."

"Stay safe, my friend. And good luck unraveling my brother's dark past."

Chapter 8

"Guess what I have?" Mrs. T's voice broke Olivia's train of thought as the older woman entered the back room, waving a notebook like it was a prized recipe. "Eleanor found this under her dresser." She thumped the notebook on the table. "It's Nathan's."

Gasps filled the air, and Lockie let out a low growl, making Olivia's arm hair stand to attention.

She reached out to touch it. "I always wondered why it wasn't mentioned in the newspaper article."

"Are there any clues about Max's accomplices or how he got in and out of the bank undetected?" Tammy asked.

"Or where the money is stashed?" Xander added, his eyes locked on the notebook.

"Remember, Nathan was convinced the money was hidden in the cavity in Tammy's fireplace, and we know that's not true," said Wally.

The team gathered around, crowding Olivia's space as Mrs. T opened the notebook and flipped through the pages.

Xander's fingers trailed the margins.

Lockie pawed at the corners and swished his tail.

The familiar comfort of her bookstore faded away as Olivia lost herself in Nathan's cramped handwriting.

"Are there any names?" she asked.

"There." Wally's finger landed on the page.

"Clark Michaels... Samuel Grey... and wait for it..." Olivia could hardly believe what she saw. "Victor Walsh..."

"As in Victor Walsh, Mary Collins's boyfriend? The one who found her body?" Xander asked.

"Victor wasn't so innocent after all," said Mrs. Temperance.

"And that's why he wasn't at dinner the night Mary died," said Olivia, "because he'd told her about the heist, and Max killed her to protect them all."

"We never officially crossed him off our suspects list. It was just that Nathan's escapades took over," said Mrs. T.

"The bones could belong to one of these three men," said Tammy.

"And one of them might have the money," Olivia said.

This was deliciously intriguing, like finding an unexpected branch on a family tree.

Pushing back from the table, Olivia grabbed her laptop. Her fingers flew across the keyboard as she logged into her genealogy accounts. This was her element—tracing lives through documents and records. "I'll trace their whereabouts after the heist in '54."

The familiar interface welcomed her as she dove into marriage and death certificates and voter records. Her brain cataloged each detail like ingredients in a complex recipe. "Clark Michaels married in 1961, moved to Florida, died in 1985. Samuel Grey stayed local, married Charlotte Adams in 1956, passed in '98."

Wally scribbled down the information. "Did she know what company her husband kept?"

"Only one way to find out," Olivia said, scanning through family trees. "I'll keep digging."

"Last but not least, our good old southpaw, Victor Walsh," Mrs. Temperance said.

Olivia paused, frowning at her screen. Victor Walsh's records were like a half-written cookbook with pages missing right where you needed them most. "Victor's trail gets interesting. He stayed in Willowcroft, but there's a gap. From 1955 to 1957 he disappears from the voting records but is there in 1954 and 1958."

"Worth investigating," Wally said, rubbing his chin. "Maybe he laid low after the heist? Or perhaps he met someone who hid the money?"

Lockie jumped onto the table, his whiskers twitching as he studied her screen. This case was marinating nicely—three new suspects, all with potential connections to Max's heist.

"Great work!" Tammy praised, patting her friend on the back. "But all were alive and well years after the bank heist. None of them are the skeleton."

"They might lead us to something else, though," Xander said.

"I've got some addresses from the death certificates," Olivia said, scribbling notes with her left hand while scrolling with her right. "The informants are usually next of kin. We might be able to trace their descendants through old phone directories at the library."

Tammy stood up. "Lockie and I are on it."

Olivia jotted down the details and passed the note to Tammy. She made a second list for Xander. "See if you can find anything online about these names and families, Xander."

"Consider it done." Xander tapped away on his computer.

Wally moved to the kitchenette. "I'll make coffee."

"And I want to read more of this notebook," said Mrs. Temperance, picking it up from beside Olivia.

Time melted away as Olivia followed digital breadcrumbs through census records and property deeds. Her shoulders had begun to ache when the bell chimed.

The door banged against the wall as Tammy burst in, papers clutched in her hand. Lockie the cat trotted behind her, tail held high like a fuzzy flagpole of feline triumph.

"I've got them!" Tammy slapped the papers down, sending a draft across Olivia's open notebook. "Names and phone numbers of potential descendants, as recent as 2016."

"Great work!" Olivia said as she began organizing the papers into neat piles for each family. "We should start making calls right away and see if anyone can help us with our investigation."

"How do we approach them without raising suspicion?" asked Tammy.

"We can try different tactics and adjust as we go," Olivia said, ruffling Lockie's ears when he headbutted her elbow. "We want information about how Max got in and out of the bank, where he hid the money, and any connections to the skeleton."

Her genealogy exploits over the years had taught her that each branch of a family held different parts of its history. Getting in touch with one branch was never enough.

Mrs. T's phone rattled against the tabletop. She glanced at it, frowned, and turned it face down.

Olivia's fingers danced across her smartphone screen as she dialed the first number on her list. She pressed the speaker button. Her fingers drummed against the wooden tabletop as the call rang. Once, twice—

"Hello?" A gruff male voice barked.

She straightened, adopting her most professional tone. "Good afternoon, sir. I'm calling about your great-uncle, Clark Michaels. We're researching Willowcroft's history and—"

"Not interested." The sharp click of disconnection stung like a slap across the face.

Heat crept up her neck. It had gone about as well as her first attempt at soufflé. Her obsession with food was always more about the eating than the baking.

Tammy exhaled. "Well, that was short-lived."

Lockie, apparently disappointed with the lack of attention, launched himself at a stack of papers. He skated across the polished tabletop, scattering documents in his wake before landing with perfect feline grace on Wally's lap.

"Rejection builds character," Olivia quipped, though her stomach churned. "Besides, we've got plenty more names to simmer."

Mrs. T's phone jolted again, skittering a few inches across the table. She snatched it up, eyes widening as she read the message before shoving it into her pocket. Her words about old bones barely registered as Olivia punched in the next number. Her fingers trembled, as they did when handling delicate documents.

"Hello?" A female voice warmed the speaker.

Olivia infused her tone with the enthusiasm she reserved for discussing rare first editions. "Hi there. I'm calling about your grandfather, Samuel Grey. We're working on a local history project, and—"

"Oh, Grandpa!"

The woman's stories poured out like honey, sweet with nostalgia. Olivia scribbled notes furiously, her glasses sliding down her nose as she captured every detail about Samuel Grey's life in Willowcroft—none of which was relevant to the case.

After they hung up, Olivia watched Tammy take the next call. The conversation crashed and burned faster than an overheated oven.

"Listen, lady, I don't know what you're after, but my family doesn't talk about him. Got it?"

Clark Michaels' grandson's voice blasted through the speaker with enough ice to freeze Hell, followed by an abrupt click of disconnection.

Wally leaned back in his chair, dislodging Lockie. "My old captain used to say, 'Time heals all wounds, but some scars refuse to fade.'"

Mrs. T's phone vibrated for the third time. She pulled it from her pocket, the glow illuminating her face with a blue-white light. Her fingers flew across the screen, tapping out a rapid response before setting it on the table, where it shuddered again.

She groaned and snatched it up.

"For heaven's sake." Mrs. T pushed herself to her feet, her chair scraping against the floor. "I'm afraid I'll have to leave you all to make the rest of these calls. Marjorie has called an emergency knitting meeting at my house since I missed the actual meeting yesterday."

Olivia stifled a smile. *You don't want to get on the wrong side of Marjorie.* Missing a meeting was tantamount to treason.

Mrs. T gathered her belongings, her movements sharp with irritation. "Marjorie's going to want all the details and will give me a dressing down as well."

"What would she even say?" Olivia asked. "Finding a body in a secret tunnel is a pretty solid excuse."

Mrs. T's lips twisted. "Marjorie reported me missing to the sheriff, remember? The woman called in the cavalry because I missed one meeting." She stuffed her still-trembling phone into her purse. "Now she's rounded up the whole circle. They'll want every detail about the skeleton, the tunnels, everything. The whole town is in a tizzy about the news."

She adjusted her bag, the phone buzzing like a trapped bee. It hadn't stopped since she stood up. "They might know about the tunnels."

The door clicked shut behind her, and Lockie claimed Mrs. T's vacant chair, turning three circles before settling in with the air of a king on a newly acquired throne.

Olivia tried to concentrate on their remaining numbers rather than Mrs. T's distracting situation.

Tracing this case was like following a stubborn family line—twisting, branching, and rarely leading where you expected.

"Okay, let's divvy up the numbers and keep going. Someone has to talk."

She dialed again, fingers crossed under the table like she used to do before major exams.

"Hello?"

Olivia slipped into her genealogist voice—the same one that had convinced countless distant relatives to share their family stories. "Hi, I'm Olivia. I'm doing some family research and believe we might share a common ancestor. Would you be open to meeting and discussing family history?"

Silence stretched, slow and uncertain, like waiting for bread to rise. Then: "Sure, I love learning about my family tree."

Success bubbled inside her chest as they arranged to meet at the Cozy Corner Café in Oaktown. One down! Her early days of archive diving had taught her that persistence always paid off.

Lockie chose that moment to spring onto her lap, nearly causing her to drop the phone. He settled himself on her thighs, tail sweeping across her notes, green eyes blinking as if to say, "You're welcome for my assistance."

She didn't pause before dialing the next number. This time, she led with Victor Walsh and the bank robbery. Sometimes you had to crack a few eggs to make an omelet, after all.

The man's hesitation spoke volumes before he admitted to family whispers. By the time they arranged to meet at his house in two days, Olivia crackled with energy. She'd been talking to Victor's son, and now they had two meetings! This case was cooking nicely.

She watched Wally make the next call, his calm voice steady while she radiated restless energy beside him. When he secured their third meeting at the Swinging Spoon the next day, Olivia wanted to dance. Three different branches of their mystery tree, all ready to bear fruit.

"Three meetings in two days?" She hugged her genealogy notebook to her chest. "That's like stumbling onto an unindexed census cache!"

Tammy stretched, her chair creaking. "Not bad for a group of amateur sleuths cold-calling about long-buried family scandals."

Olivia smirked. *Amateur sleuths, professional nuisances. That should go on a business card.* "I'd say we're off to a great start."

Chapter 9

Hazel sighed as she stepped out of Sweet Crumbs, balancing Mrs. Applewood's award-winning, warm apple pie. The Willow-Crafters would expect to be fed even at an emergency meeting. Marjorie would scold her for skipping the last one, Betty would fuss over whether she'd eaten enough, and Della Mae would take out her knitting needles and click away in judgment.

Sure enough, as Hazel crossed the square toward her home, she spotted Marjorie and Betty standing on her porch.

"There she is!" Marjorie declared, throwing her hands in the air. "Alive and well! Which is more than I can say for the skeleton she found!"

Hazel groaned. "You rang Sheriff Stanton because I missed a knitting meeting?"

Betty clutched her chest. "We thought something had happened to you! You never miss."

"I was busy finding a skeleton." Hazel stepped past them, unlocking the door. "You'd think that would give me some leeway."

"Oh, it does," Marjorie said, breezing inside as if she owned the place. "Which is why we need details. The whole town's talking about it."

By the time Beatrice and Della Mae arrived, Hazel had tea steeping, the pie plated, and was bracing herself for the full force of knitting-circle speculation. Beatrice had pulled out her latest knitting project, a scarf developing a lace pattern due to her ongoing trouble with the slip stitch.

"What's happening?" she asked, frowning at the tangled yarn.

"You're dropping stitches again," Hazel said, examining it. "Here, let me—"

"So," Marjorie began, "who do we think the skeleton is?"

"Not one of us, obviously," Hazel said.

"I mean historically speaking!" Marjorie huffed. "Someone local? Or an out-of-towner? A criminal? A wronged lover?"

"Ooh, a wronged lover," Betty said dreamily. "Perhaps a scandalous affair, a tragic end—"

"Betty," Hazel cut in, "we don't even know if it's a man or a woman."

"Well, how long does it take for a body to become a skeleton?" Della Mae asked. "That might tell us if it's from the heist or earlier."

"Oh, let's look it up!" Betty said, pulling out her phone and peering at it like it was a relic from another world. "Xander showed me how to search for things."

"This should be good," Hazel muttered, sipping her tea.

Betty squinted at the screen. "Okay, I type it in here, and... oh. Oh dear."

Marjorie leaned over. "What did you search?"

Betty's face turned pink. "Well, I meant to write 'how long does it take for a body to become a skeleton' but... I may have left out a few words, and now I have, uh, something about dieting tips and... is this an ad for a mortuary?"

Beatrice cackled. "Here, let me try." She tapped at her phone with great concentration. "Oh dear, now it says 'how long does it take for a skeleton to grow skin.' That's not what I wanted."

Whoop. Whoop.

Della Mae's phone blared to life, making everyone jump.

"Goodness gracious!" Della Mae exclaimed, fumbling with her phone as it continued making growling noises. "What on earth is happening?"

Betty peered over. "The Willowcroft Campground bear cam!"

"Bear cam?" Hazel asked, moving to look.

Della Mae held her phone, showing a black bear scratching its back against a pine tree. "Xander created some alert system that sends me a notification whenever a bear appears on the camera."

"How thoughtful," Marjorie said dryly. "Nothing says 'thinking of you' like live bear alerts."

Della Mae huffed. "I find it useful! Last month, I called Ranger Dan when I saw two cubs without a mama bear nearby. Turns out they were just playing while she was fishing, but—better safe than sorry!"

"Is that what all those dings were during our last meeting?" Hazel asked. "I thought you were texting someone the whole time."

"Oh no, I'm not that good at it yet, dear. It was an active bear day," Della Mae said, watching the screen with fascination. "How about this big fellow! Must be getting ready for hibernation. Xander says I can take screenshots, but I haven't quite figured it out."

"Let me try," Betty offered, reaching for the phone—only to swipe away from the bear cam.

"Oh! Dell!" she squeaked, yanking her hand back as if she'd touched a hot stove.

Mrs. T blinked. That wasn't a bear.

Della Mae snatched the phone back, her cheeks flushing. "That's not... Xander must have... I would never..."

Marjorie snorted. "My, my. Bear watching isn't the only hobby you've picked up, is it?"

"It was an ad! It just popped up!" Della Mae protested, swiping at her screen.

Marjorie snatched the phone. "Let me—how did I end up on a website selling Halloween decorations?"

"This is why I still use my encyclopedias," Beatrice declared.

"While you're waging war on the internet, I'll tell you what I know," Hazel said, rescuing the conversation. "The tunnels stretch from under the Swinging Spoon—back when it was the apothecary. We found a cocktail symbol carved into the basement door, marking the entrance to a speakeasy. And, of course, where we found the skeleton. But there are also smaller passages veering off in all directions. It wouldn't surprise me if there were more entrances under other buildings in town."

"Oh, Mrs. Hubbard's Cupboard!" Marjorie exclaimed. "My mother-in-law always said you got flour and sugar and a little something extra if you knocked on the back door with the right code word."

Beatrice raised an eyebrow. "No wonder it survived through the Depression and beyond."

Betty perked up. "Oh, did I ever tell you my grandparents met in a speakeasy?"

Marjorie smirked. "That explains your romantic proclivities."

Betty beamed. "Grandpa always said he saw Grandma across the room, sipping 'giggle water' and laughing like she owned the place. He found the courage to ask her to dance, and done—love at first sight."

"Did your grandfather ever share any of the 'lingo' they used back then?" Della Mae asked, setting her knitting down. "My aunt Mildred taught me that proper ladies never got drunk—they only got 'zozzled' on special occasions."

"Oh, yes!" Betty nodded. "Grandma would talk about the 'mixologist' who made the best cocktails in the county. Though she admitted once that when the 'heat' was rumored to be snooping around, everyone was too 'ossified' to find the exit!"

"Our town's speakeasy was quite the engineering marvel," Marjorie added, reaching for another slice of pie. "Being in tunnels meant people came and went without being spotted on the street. I've heard other towns had places behind fake walls or through freezers, but nothing as elaborate as an entire underground network like what we have."

"It was about more than drinking," Della Mae noted. "In speakeasies, women were able to let loose for the first time. Respectable ladies wouldn't dream of being seen with a cocktail in public."

"True," Beatrice said. "Women's hemlines went up, corsets came off, and everyone bobbed their hair and wore rouge in public."

Hazel helped herself to more apple pie. "Makes me wonder if our skeleton ties into all the social change. What if it was someone who didn't want things changing? Or someone trying to protect their covert world?"

"Or maybe," Beatrice said, "it was someone who knew too much about who was drinking what with whom. In a small town like this, a speakeasy wasn't just about alcohol. It was private meetings, affairs, business deals made under the table..."

Hazel refocused on her knitting. "It's so interesting. Our quiet little town had a whole underground life nobody talks about. Literally underground, as it turns out." She shook her head. "But I'm more concerned with figuring out who the skeleton was."

Della Mae, still struggling with her slip stitch, sighed. "I don't know about love stories and speakeasies, but I do know I'll never finish this scarf at this rate."

Betty set down her phone. "Even if we never uncover the identity, it's nice to think of all the stories these tunnels must hold."

Hazel rubbed her temples. "I think I need a drink."

"Go knock on the back of Mrs. Hubbard's Cupboard," Marjorie suggested with a grin. "You never know."

Chapter 10

Bookworm Haven set aside Thursday mornings for toddler storytime, otherwise known as Bookworm Wigglers. Olivia perched on her wooden stool, holding today's selection—*The Bouncy Bear's Big Adventure*. A semi-circle of squirming toddlers wobbled on the soft storytime rug, their chubby hands clutching sippy cups and half-eaten crackers. It was one of her favorite times of the week.

The team was meeting with the suspects' descendants today, and here she was, corralling toddlers instead of correlating evidence. *But these weekly readings are as much a part of me now as my genealogy research.*

She sold a lot of books after each reading. Storytime was good for the soul and business, which justified taking time away from the case. The beauty of teamwork. *One person sifts flour while another beats eggs, and somehow you still end up with a cake. Or so I've been told.*

Olivia smiled. "Everyone ready?"

A few enthusiastic nods, a few distracted pokes at a neighbor's shoe, and one child, Jackson, already bouncing in place, which was... fitting, given the title.

Olivia pressed on. "'And then the bear bounced so high—'" She lifted her hands dramatically.

Jackson sprang to his feet.

"BOUNCE!" he squealed.

Oh no.

Before Olivia could stop it, the other toddlers took this as their cue. One by one, they launched into the air, giggling, wobbling, and crashing into each other like a tiny stampede of enthusiastic kangaroos.

If these kids found the murder board tucked away in my back room, they'd probably tear it apart, ruining our plotted timelines and suspect photos. Though knowing Jackson, he'd solve the case in the chaos. The next Sherlock Holmes might be wearing pull-ups and a juice-stained shirt.

"Okay, okay! Let's settle back down—"

Too late.

Jackson, caught in his own momentum, wobbled toward the bookstore's front window and smacked both hands against the glass. Another child followed. Then another. Within seconds, half the group had joined the window-pounding rebellion.

BANG.

BANG.

BANG.

Mothers sprang from their chairs like startled deer. Olivia's stomach lurched.

"Jackson, honey, step away from the—"

CRASH.

A loud tinkle of glass showered onto the sidewalk. Olivia's breath caught in her throat. The toddlers froze. The parents froze. For a single, perfect second, absolute silence filled the store.

Then Jackson's voice rang out.

"Bookstore broke!"

Olivia squeezed her eyes shut. Not out of fear—no one was hurt—but out of sheer, overwhelming exhaustion.

Of course this happened.

Of course toddlers had just bodily removed her front window.

And of course, now she'd have to call Mike, again.

At the thought of the broad-shouldered glazier, Olivia swallowed hard. Not that she had a crush on him. *She didn't.* Don't be ridiculous. She barely noticed how his tool belt sat snugly against his waist or how his sleeves were always pushed up enough to show his forearms.

No thoughts about that. None.

Was this the universe's way of giving her what she wanted? With the store closed for repairs, she'd have time to join the descendants' meetings. *Sometimes good things come wrapped in broken glass and property damage.*

A mother groaned into her scarf. "I *knew* storytime was getting too rowdy."

Another was already reaching for her wallet. "I'll cover the damages, Olivia."

Olivia shook her head, snapping herself back to reality. "No, no. No one's paying for anything. It was an accident." *A very... enthusiastic accident.*

She surveyed the wide-eyed parents and the toddlers, who had already moved on and were now trying to chase Lockie under a bookshelf.

Her gaze landed on Jackson, still beaming, his cheeks smooshed against what remained of the window.

Olivia sighed. "Well, since we had such a *memorable* storytime today, everyone gets a free copy of the book!"

The tension in the room dissipated.

"Oh, how generous."

"Thank you, Olivia."

"Jackson, say thank you."

"Taaank yoooou!" Jackson chirped, as if he had done everyone a favor by bringing the structural integrity of the bookstore into question.

Next week's storytime should feature a book about sitting still.

As the parents herded their toddlers out, Olivia took a slow, deep breath and pulled out her phone. *Time to call Mike.*

Not that she was looking forward to it or anything. Nope. Not at all.

Now she could marinate in thoughts about Mike and the case. Nothing like a broken window to clear one's schedule. She'd have to move fast if she wanted to catch up with the team's progress on the descendants' interviews. Her stomach fluttered with equal parts anticipation about both prospects.

Chapter 11

Olivia breathed in the comforting scent of cinnamon and coffee as she and Tammy stepped inside the Cozy Corner Café in Oaktown. The broken front window had forced her to close the bookstore for the day, which allowed her to attend the meeting. Wally, Mrs. T, and Xander had agreed to watch the place while she was gone.

A woman sat alone near the window. Olivia guessed correctly that it was Rebecca Grey.

She stirred her tea, watching the amber liquid swirl as she considered her approach. This was like opening a new family history: you had to start gently.

"Rebecca, thank you for meeting with us," Olivia said, still stirring. "We're trying to piece together some information on an old bank heist in Willowcroft seventy years ago."

Rebecca's cappuccino left a foam mustache, which she quickly wiped away. "Fascinating. But what does that have to do with my family tree?"

Olivia let Tammy explain about Max Cross and Samuel Grey's potential involvement while she studied the young woman's reaction, her eyes widening with each revelation like pages in a book suddenly thrown open.

Rebecca leaned forward. "My family always had this legend about my great-uncle being involved in a bank heist, but nobody took it seriously. I never thought it could be true!"

Olivia's heart quickened. Family legends were like recipe cards passed through generations—the basic ingredients stayed the same, even if the measurements got fuzzy.

"Can you tell us more about your family legend?" she asked, pen poised.

She scribbled notes as Rebecca shared the tale. A daring heist in darkness, money stashed away—it was as vague as a recipe saying *"some flour"* and *"cook until done"* for instructions. Still, it added weight to their suspicions.

Rebecca's head tilted as her fingers twisted a loose thread on her sleeve. "I have a distant cousin on that side of the family, Elaine, who's been obsessed with genealogy for years and even traveled to some archives in other states."

Olivia perked up. "Would you mind sharing her contact information?"

Rebecca pressed her lips into a thin line. "I don't think she'd appreciate me giving out her number to strangers. Elaine's pretty protective of her privacy." She tapped her fingers on the table. "But I can reach out to her myself and ask her to contact you."

"Perfect," Olivia said, sliding one of her genealogy business cards across the table. One thing Olivia had learned over the years is that even private people talk with fellow genealogists.

Rebecca tucked the card into her purse. "She's been collecting old family papers and photographs for years. If anyone would know more about this heist, it's Elaine."

"Wonderful," Tammy said, exchanging a quick, hopeful glance with Olivia.

Rebecca stood to leave. "I can't promise she'll call. She can be... selective about what family history she shares, but it's worth a try."

"Thank you, Rebecca," Olivia said as their meeting ended. "Your insights have been invaluable." *Though not going to solve our mystery.*

"Happy to help!" Rebecca replied before departing.

"Let's hope Elaine calls soon," said Tammy. "Sounds like she's the one we need to talk to."

"Family researchers like her often have folders of information the rest of the family never hears about."

"Let's hope she's not holding out because she's sitting on a pile of stolen money," Tammy joked.

"In my experience, family stories come from actual occurrences, though they get as mixed up as a badly folded recipe card through the generations." She shared one of her favorite examples—the romantic tale of the heartbroken widower, which was more scandal than romance. It reminded her why she loved genealogy—every family tree had its share of surprising ingredients.

Tammy grinned. "Do you ever get nervous telling your clients what you find?"

"The hardest one was when I told a priest his grandmother was born out of wedlock." Olivia checked her watch and jumped.

And speaking of unexpected surprises...

"I need to get back to the store. The glazier's coming this afternoon to fix the window." Her heart did a little flip as she wondered if Mike would be the one coming.

She didn't care, of course. Much.

She gathered her things, pushing thoughts of a certain handsome glazier aside and trying to focus on the case instead.

One descendant seemed particularly excited to meet with them: a young woman named Emily Michaels, a direct descendant of Clark Michaels.

Wally had arranged a meeting at the Swinging Spoon and invited Mrs. T to join him, hoping Emily would be more at ease with another woman present.

They settled into their regular booth and waited.

A young girl walked in, barely out of her teens, and scanned the diner. Wally waved. "Emily?"

The woman smiled and headed in their direction.

"Thank you so much for meeting with me!" the young women said as she settled into the bench seat opposite. "I've always been fascinated by our family history, and when you mentioned the possibility of a bank heist connection, I couldn't wait to share what little I know about this legend and hear what you have to say."

"Please," Mrs. Temperance said, "tell us everything."

"All right," Emily began, scooting to the edge of the booth's seat. "So, from what I've gathered, my great-grandfather Clark Michaels was allegedly involved in this bank heist. It's been passed down through the generations as a family story, but nobody ever had the specifics."

"Interesting," Wally said, taking notes. "And do you have any idea who the other people involved might have been?"

"No," Emily replied with a sigh. "My family only ever mentioned Clark's involvement, and that there may have been others. But no one knew their identities, at least not to my knowledge."

"Do you have any idea what happened with the money?" Wally asked, scrutinizing Emily's reaction. "It was never recovered."

She shrugged. "My family saw none of it. There are no rich uncles I'm aware of. I'm collecting student debt like you wouldn't believe."

It was clear they would not get any answers from Emily. She was hoping to get answers from them. *Maybe we'll have more luck tomorrow.*

The bookstore sat silent and empty, the new window gleaming in the light from the street lamps. Mike had done an excellent job—not that she'd been watching him work all afternoon, stealing glances while pretending to organize inventory nearby. He'd even stayed a few minutes after finishing to admire her collection of first editions, his appreciation for craftsmanship extending beyond glass to binding and typography. When he'd left with a promise to "check in soon to make sure the window's settling," she'd found herself looking forward to his return.

Olivia stacked three misplaced books on the proper shelf, then paused. The half-swept floor and knocked-over brochure carousel glared at her. She should finish cleaning and prepare to reopen.

But the murder board called to her like a warm slice of pie, impossible to resist.

She abandoned her restocking and ducked into the back room, where the table stood covered in their collected evidence. Faces of suspects and victims stared at her, connected by red yarn and wild theories. She flipped open her laptop. The Grey family historian, cousin Elaine, hadn't contacted them, but it had given Olivia an idea.

Her fingers tapped across the keyboard, filling the search bar with various combinations of "Samuel Grey," "historian," and "Elaine Grey." Family historians never just kept records to themselves—they published, shared, and bragged about their discoveries.

"Come on, Elaine," Olivia muttered, scrolling through another page of search results. "Show me what you found."

The fifth page of results made her sit up straight. A book title blazed across the screen like a beacon: *Bootleggers and Bandits: The Michaels Family in Prohibition Michigan.*

"Bingo!" Olivia scooted her chair closer, her pulse quickening as she devoured the description. The Michaels family had built a small empire during Prohibition, complete with speakeasies, rumrunners, and—Olivia squealed—rumored bank heists. And there were references to the Grey and Walsh families.

Olivia clicked "Add to Cart" faster than she grabbed a chocolate chip cookie fresh from the oven. This book might contain the answers they'd been searching for—the tunnel connections, the missing money, perhaps even the identity of their skeleton.

She entered her payment information, mentally calculating how long it would take to read the entire book once it arrived. *Why wasn't there a sample or at least a contents page?*

The confirmation email dinged into her inbox. Olivia clicked it open, already eager to share this breakthrough with the team.

Estimated delivery: Two weeks from today.

Her excitement deflated like a collapsed sponge cake.

Olivia slumped in her chair. Two weeks might as well be two centuries when it came to solving murders and bank robberies.

She closed the laptop with a snap. There was no sense in getting the others' hopes up only to make them wait. Better to keep this lead to herself for now.

Chapter 12

The next morning, they met at the bookstore to plan their day.

"Mrs. Temperance and I will meet with Peter Walsh so Olivia can get the store ready to reopen," said Tammy.

"Xander and I will help and then keep researching," said Wally.

The Walsh house was a few blocks behind the square. As they approached the front door, they were greeted by a middle-aged man with graying hair and a forced smile.

"Hello! You must be Tammy and Mrs. Temperance," he said, extending his hand. "Olivia told me you'd be coming. I'm Peter Walsh, Victor's youngest son. Come on in, I've been looking forward to chatting with you."

"Thank you for having us, Peter," Mrs. Temperance replied as they entered a living room cluttered with furniture. The smell of baking cookies and something more pungent wafted from the kitchen.

"Are you a baker?" Mrs. T asked. "Something smells... delicious?"

"No. No. My youngest daughter Rachel's the chef of the family." He glanced toward the kitchen as if expecting someone or something to emerge.

As they settled into their seats, Tammy asked, "So, what can you tell us about your father Victor and his connection to the bank heist?"

"Well, I have to admit I don't know a whole lot," Peter said, rubbing the back of his neck. "My father didn't talk about himself much. But I'd be more than happy to learn along with you."

"Every bit of information helps," Mrs. Temperance assured him. "Perhaps there are some old documents or photographs we could see."

"I have a box of old things belonging to Victor," Peter said, a strange tightness in his expression. "I'd be happy to share them if you promise to keep me updated on any discoveries you make."

"Of course," Tammy agreed, her curiosity piqued.

Peter's gaze swept the room. "I've heard so many rumors, and I'd love the truth." His hands fidgeted in his lap.

Why is he so eager? He's acting like one of my characters when they are hiding something. What isn't he telling us?

"We'd be more than happy to share our findings with you," said Tammy.

Something's off. She turned toward the kitchen. A flash of an apron behind the half-open pocket door. Rachel? *Why isn't she joining us?*

A clang came from another room, not the kitchen.

Tammy straightened.

Is someone else here?

"I'm curious," Tammy said. "Where was Victor during the years 1955 to 1957?"

A glass shattered in the kitchen. Peter jumped.

"Sorry!" called a female voice—Rachel, presumably.

Tammy kept her tone neutral. "He doesn't seem to have been in Willowcroft."

Peter cleared his throat. "Those years? I, uh...I believe he traveled. For work. Or family business. It was before my time."

Tammy caught Mrs. Temperance's eye. The older woman's lips pressed into a tight line.

"I'll grab the box." Peter pushed himself up from his chair and disappeared into a back room.

Tammy strained her ears at the sound of hushed voices. Male voices. Two of them, whispering from the direction Peter had gone.

"...can't..."

"...no..."

"...the photos..."

The whispers stopped. Peter returned, box in hand, his smile too wide, too forced. Sweat beaded at his hairline despite the cool temperature in the room.

"Here we are," he announced, his voice an octave higher than before. "Just some old mementos."

His hands trembled as he handed over the worn cardboard box filled with yellowed papers and tattered photographs.

Was it reluctance, nervousness, excitement?

Tammy scanned the room again. Peter... and Rachel in the kitchen. And the second male voice?

"Thank you for this," Mrs. Temperance said, rising to her feet. "We should let you get back to your day."

Tammy and Mrs. Temperance thanked him and took their leave.

"Weird," said Tammy. "Peter seemed too eager to part with his father's belongings. It's not every day someone lets go of family heirlooms, especially to strangers. And those voices—did you hear them?"

Mrs. Temperance's bun bobbed as she agreed. "Two men arguing over the box? But Peter only mentioned his daughter being there."

"And did you notice how they reacted when I mentioned 1955 to 1957? Something happened during those years." Tammy clutched the box of documents to her chest. "Let's get these back to the team. I'll bet there's something in here someone doesn't want us to see."

She peeked over her shoulder at the house. A curtain in the upper window fell into place.

Upon entering the bookstore, Tammy and Mrs. Temperance found Olivia serving a customer while Wally and Xander restocked the tourist information brochure carousel in the reinstated window. "I'm so glad the, what is it—the third broken window?—hasn't deterred the customers."

Olivia chuckled. "Oh, don't remind me. Three broken windows in six weeks. At this rate, I might as well book the glazier in for two weeks' time. I'm excellent business for Mike."

"Oh? Mike, is it? Not Mr. Leeman anymore?"

Olivia busied herself with straightening a stack of paperbacks and avoiding eye contact as her cheeks reddened. "After the second window incident, we got to talking. He's quite knowledgeable about, um, glass."

Wally suppressed a grin as he slotted another brochure into place. "I'm sure he is."

Olivia's blush deepened, spreading to the tips of her ears. She busied herself organizing a stack of bookmarks on the counter.

"Mmhmm," Mrs. Temperance hummed. "And I suppose you haven't noticed his rugged good looks and charming smile."

"What's in the box?" Xander asked, changing the subject to Olivia's obvious relief.

Tammy set the box on the counter with a thud. "Peter Walsh gave us these family papers and photos, but something about it was off."

"How so?" Wally abandoned the brochure rack and moved closer.

"He practically shoved the box at us like he couldn't get rid of it fast enough," Mrs. Temperance said, her lips thinning. "And when Tammy asked about Victor's whereabouts between 1955 and 1957—"

"A glass shattered in the kitchen," Tammy finished. "Rachel said it was nothing, but I don't think she was alone."

"There were voices," Mrs. Temperance added. "Two male voices. But Peter only mentioned his daughter."

Tammy glanced at the front window. "And someone was watching from upstairs when we left. Whoever it was didn't want us there."

Wally stroked his chin. "Sounds like someone didn't want the box leaving the house."

"Well then," Olivia said. "Let's go through it. To the back room!"

With no more customers in the store, they retreated to their secret lair.

As Tammy and Mrs. Temperance removed the contents from the box, Olivia and Wally began sorting through the various documents and albums. The musty smell prompted a sneeze from Lockie. The feline companion rubbed against Tammy's leg, seeking comfort amidst the flurry of activity.

"There's all sorts of things in here." Wally spread several yellowed papers across the table. "Birth certificates, old letters, newspaper clippings."

Xander, ever the tech-savvy teenager, set up a projector to scan the photographs. "If someone didn't want us to see these, there must be something important."

"Focus on anything from those years I mentioned," Tammy said, pulling out a leather-bound album. "1955 to 1957. Those dates triggered something in that house."

"Watch out for anyone who might be the mystery man," Mrs. Temperance added. "If Peter wasn't alone with his daughter, who was the second man, and why hide from us?"

"But not even Rachel joined us, to be fair," said Tammy.

"True," replied Mrs. T.

Olivia picked up a stack of envelopes tied with a faded ribbon. "The plot thickens, doesn't it? Our little investigation just got more interesting."

"And potentially dangerous," Wally said. "If they're hiding something, they might not appreciate us digging."

Tammy paused, a photograph half-removed from its envelope. "All the more reason to find out what it is."

"Look at this," Olivia called out, holding an old photograph of three men. "Are these our three suspects—Clark Michaels, Samuel Grey, and Victor Walsh?"

"Quite possible," Wally agreed, leaning in. "We should cross-reference this with other sources to confirm their identities."

"I'll put it on the projector," Xander suggested, adjusting his glasses. As the image appeared on the wall, each member of the team gathered around, scrutinizing every detail and speculating on its significance.

The three men were dressed in the fashion of the 1950s. Their expressions were serious, but a glimmer in their eyes hinted at shared confidences.

"They seem to fit the time period, and they're close in age."

"Where's Max, though?" Wally asked, scanning the picture for any sign of the infamous criminal. "He'd have been younger than these guys, right?"

"Maybe he took the picture," Xander added.

"True," Mrs. Temperance replied. "But Max may not have been part of their inner circle."

"Let's not jump to conclusions yet," Olivia cautioned, her brows knitting together in thought. "We need more information about these men and the connection between them and Max."

Lockie, the ever-present feline companion, sauntered into the room and leaped onto the table, surveying the papers and photos strewn across the surface. He emitted a soft purr, seemingly content to be part of the brainstorming process.

Tammy sifted through the documents and came across an envelope. She pulled out a delicate piece of paper and gasped at what she saw.

"Guys, I've found a letter signed 'Mary.' Could this be Mary Collins?"

"Mary and Victor dated," said Olivia.

"And we never crossed Victor off our suspect list?" said Mrs. T. "I knew there was more to the story."

Chapter 13

Olivia suggested yet another novel to a regular customer until the entry bell chimed. She peered around the stacks to see Tammy juggling Sweet Crumbs boxes. "Sustenance has arrived," Tammy said. "And so too has the mail." Her head bobbed toward an envelope sitting atop one of the boxes.

"But Mr. Taylor has already delivered the mail."

"I found it wedged under the door. I don't think this one came via the postal service."

"Is it for me?" Olivia's curiosity was palpable.

"It doesn't say."

Mrs. Wright's peaceful browsing sounds drifted from the historical fiction section. Olivia had cataloged this particular customer's habits like a well-researched family tree—she was only on browse number two of her usual three before purchase. "Mrs. Wright? I'll be in the back if you need me."

"All good, dear," came the response, muffled by shelves.

"Do you need to stay?" asked Tammy.

Olivia shook her head, already moving toward the disguised door. "No. Mrs. Wright's as predictable as a library catalog. She won't be purchasing today."

The bookcase door took them into their investigation room, where the rest of the team was working.

Xander made a beeline for the food boxes. *Teenagers are hungry creatures.*

Tammy waved the envelope. "Someone's been writing to us."

"Careful," Wally said as he studied the unexpected delivery. "Might be anything."

"A clue," said Xander with his mouth full. "Or a warning, which means we might be close to something."

"Or junk mail," said Mrs. T.

Olivia's fingers itched to grab the envelope and examine every detail.

Tammy slid the edge of a letter opener beneath the sealed flap.

"It's a newspaper article." Paper from the *Stonefield Times*, dated 1954, lay spread across their table. The headline hit Olivia like a sour bomb candy: Another Bank Heist in Greater Willowcroft: Stonefield Mutual Latest Victim.

"The similarities to the Willowcroft robbery are striking," said Wally.

"We know the Cross family moved to Stonefield. The Cross Construction Company built the plaza," said Mrs. Temperance.

Which is next to the bank. This was better than finding an unexpected marriage certificate in a family search.

"Are we uncovering a ring of criminals?" said Xander.

Does Stonefield have tunnels too? Do they connect to Willowcroft's?

Wally's stern voice anchored Olivia back to reality. "We need to dig deeper into this. Xander, any chance the Stonefield newspapers are online?"

After a few clicks, Xander said, "No, but they are available to view at the library itself."

Wally dashed out before anyone suggested joining him, leaving them with more questions than answers. Like a family tree, each answer seemed to sprout three new mysteries.

Wally arrived at the library as a few patrons were leaving.

He approached the librarian's desk. "Excuse me," he said, trying to keep his voice low enough not to disturb the hushed atmosphere. *Am I the only one here?* "I'm looking for newspaper archives from 1954. Could you point me in the right direction, please?"

The librarian gestured toward the back corner. "You'll find the microfilm machines and archives over there."

"Thank you," Wally said with a grateful nod, making his way over to the designated area.

He settled in, threading the film onto the machine.

Time slipped by as he scrolled through grainy newspaper archives, scanning for anything useful. His vision blurred, and his eyes burned something fierce. He shifted in the hard library chair, his back protesting like it did in his stakeout days.

Hold on a minute.

He double-checked the dates, working backward and forward through the archives. Nothing. No bank heist, no robbery reports, not even a whiff of suspicious activity. The article tip-off? Didn't exist.

Time to break it down like a case file: Someone had gone to considerable effort to create a fake. But who in blazes would...?

The realization hit him harder than a Southie bar brawl. This wasn't misdirection—it was tactical separation. Divide and conquer, the oldest trick in the book.

"Sweet bejeezers." He lunged for his phone, needing to warn the others.

A pulse of pain reverberated through his skull.

His vision blurred.

Darkness.

Coming to was like climbing out of molasses. How long had he been playing Sleeping Beauty? The library sat dark and quiet as a tomb, and he'd seen enough of those in Homicide to know. Sticky warmth matted his hair, and his probing fingers came away red. Blunt force trauma from behind. Textbook takedown.

"Let's examine the facts," he mumbled, forcing himself to think like the detective he'd been for thirty years. Phone: gone. Weapon of opportunity, probably. Perp knew the layout, timed it perfect.

Fighting a wave of nausea, Wally gripped the microfiche reader, steadying himself. *One step at a time, old man.*

The walk to the front desk dragged like a foot chase through Fenway—with lead in his shoes and ice picks in his skull.

Each step sent fresh pain through his head, but he'd worked through worse. He had to reach the others, make sure they hadn't walked into a trap.

"Hello?" His voice croaked. Empty. Silent. Black spots danced at the edges of his vision.

Wally's knees buckled.

The floor rushed to meet him.

As consciousness slipped away again, one thought burned through the fog: the others better be okay, or someone was gonna answer to him, concussion or no concussion.

"Sir? Sir, can you hear me?"

A voice pierced through the haze like a dispatch call on his old police radio. Wally forced his eyelids open. The librarian's concerned face swam into focus.

"What..." His tongue was thick, clumsy, like cold chowder. Instinct kicked in: assess the situation, establish timeline, identify threats. Basic detective work, even with his brain rattled like it had gone ten rounds with Sugar Ray Leonard.

"Don't move, sir. I've called an ambulance." The librarian's hands hovered. "I found you here when I was locking up."

Locking up? Blazes, how long had he been out? His phone. The team. The setup. It all came rushing back. The perp had played them like a corner con man, and here he was, flat on his back while his people could be experiencing who knows what.

"My phone," he rasped, trying to push himself up. The room tilted like he'd had one too many at the Blarney Tap. "Need to contact... my team..."

"Now, now," the librarian pressed gently on his shoulder. "The paramedics will be here any minute. You're in no shape to be playing the hero."

Playing the hero? If she'd worked Homicide for twenty years, she'd understand. Team safety always came first. But his body was betraying him worse than an informant in witness protection. The pain in his skull throbbed with each heartbeat.

The wailing sirens outside brought a sense of déjà vu. How many times had he been on the other side of this scenario? The paramedics burst in. Their movements coordinated, like as a well-executed raid.

"What's the situation?" The female paramedic's tone was pure business. Reminded him of his old partner, Sandra Jacks—never fazed by anything. *What's she up to now?*

"Found him unconscious," the librarian reported, sounding like she was giving testimony. "Disoriented with a head injury."

The paramedics worked with mechanical precision, their hands gentle but firm as they assessed him. "Possible concussion. We'll need to take him to the hospital," stated the male paramedic.

As they lifted him onto the gurney, Wally tried to maintain consciousness by working through the problem. The fake. The ambush. The phone. This wasn't random. This was calculated, planned.

"My friends," he mumbled. "Need to warn..."

"We'll take care of that, sir," the female paramedic assured him. "Stay still."

They wheeled him out into the cool night air, the flashing lights blinding him. As the ambulance sped toward the hospital, panic gnawed at his gut. Were the others safe? Had they realized something was wrong? He had to reach them.

"Something doesn't feel right." Olivia clutched her phone. Lockie let out a soft meow and rubbed against her leg.

The clock struck eight. Olivia called Wally, but straight to voicemail again. The team exchanged anxious glances.

"Wally would never ignore our calls like this," said Tammy.

"Should we call the sheriff?" asked Mrs. Temperance.

"He might be deep in research and lost track of time," said Olivia.

"The library closed two hours ago," said Xander.

The hospital room's fluorescent lights flickered and droned, harsh as an interrogation lamp. Exhaustion weighed on his battered body. Pain meds dulled the throb but hadn't eased his troubled mind.

The wall clock ticked. Midnight. The local deputies had wrapped their questioning, though he hadn't given them much. Whole thing was hazier than a Fenway fog. Amateur hour, that's what it was, getting blindsided like some rookie.

All he thought about was reaching the others.

Wally shifted his legs out of the bed, wincing at the movement. The thought of his friends scared and in potential danger was far worse than any pain.

Wally found the nurses' station.

"Please, I need to call my friends."

The nurse took pity, offering him the desk phone. "Five minutes. Then it's back to bed, or I'll have to write you up." Her attempt at cop humor wasn't lost on him.

Wally thanked her and wracked his brain to remember the number for Bookworm Haven. It rang.

Click.

"Hello?" Olivia's anxious voice greeted him.

"Olivia, it's me."

"Wally!"

He flinched, holding the phone away from his ear.

"You're alive! We've been so worried. What happened?"

Wally explained the attack. "I'll be discharged in the morning. Are you all okay?"

"Yes, we're fine."

Mrs. T's familiar snoring carried through the receiver. A comforting sound. They were safe.

"Get some rest. We'll come get you first thing."

Wally hung up. The night nurse appeared at his elbow. She steadied him as he made his way back to the room. He settled into bed, finally able to rest easy.

Olivia gripped her phone long after the call ended, her knuckles turning white. Midnight had come and gone, leaving them huddled in the back room of Bookworm Haven.

"Was that Wally?" Tammy straightened from where she'd been dozing against the wall.

"He's alive." Olivia set the phone on the cluttered table, the plastic clattering against the wood. Her fingers shook. "Someone attacked him at the library. His phone taken."

Images flashed through her mind—Wally lying on the library floor, blood pooling, no one around to help. She swallowed hard against the rising nausea. Should they continue searching or leave things be?

Xander lifted his head from the table, blinking away sleep. His glasses sat crooked on his nose. "Is it bad?"

"Hospital's keeping him overnight." Olivia glanced at Mrs. Temperance, who snored in the overstuffed armchair, her shawl draped across her like a makeshift blanket.

"Should we wake her?" Tammy whispered.

Olivia shook her head. "Let her sleep. There's nothing we can do until morning anyway."

"Did he say who did it?" Xander asked.

"No. It happened too fast." Olivia's hands trembled. She tucked them under her arms. This wasn't supposed to happen. Not to Wally. Not to any of them. They were supposed to be solving a historical mystery, not putting their lives at risk. "Someone doesn't want us digging into this skeleton."

Tammy pulled her cardigan tighter. "This isn't some cozy mystery novel. This is real. Someone hurt Wally."

"Because he found something." Xander's voice dropped to a whisper. "Something in the newspapers."

Mrs. T stirred, mumbling something about tunnels before settling back into her rhythmic snoring.

"We shouldn't have let him go alone." Olivia's throat tightened. The bookstore, usually a haven, was suddenly too quiet, too open. Every shadow seemed to stretch toward them, every creak of the building a potential threat. The realization that danger had found its way into their lives—into her life—made Olivia's skin prickle. Was someone watching the bookstore right now? Waiting for them to separate?

She crossed to the window, checking the lock. "We're not safe."

"We're safer together." Tammy joined her, pulling the blinds shut. "No one's going anywhere tonight."

Xander stood, stretching his lanky frame. "I'll check the doors."

"I'll get blankets and pillows." Olivia ran upstairs to her apartment and returned with an armful of blankets, distributing them without a word.

They moved furniture, transforming the back room into a makeshift camp. Mrs. T slept through it all.

"Someone tried to kill him." The words escaped Olivia's lips without permission.

Tammy froze mid-motion, blanket clutched in her fists. "Don't say that."

"We have to face facts." Olivia spread a blanket on the floor beside Mrs. T's chair. "Someone attacked an ex-sheriff. They weren't just trying to scare him."

"Which means we're onto something big." Xander settled into a chair.

"Or something dangerous." Tammy curled into a ball on her makeshift bed.

Olivia sat cross-legged on her blanket. The line between amateur sleuthing and real danger had vanished. Backing away wouldn't erase what happened to Wally, and it wouldn't protect them if someone believed they knew too much already.

Mrs. T's snoring stuttered, then resumed at a lower volume.

"We need a plan," Xander said. "No more splitting up."

"Agreed," Olivia replied.

"He won't like that." Tammy's lips quirked into a small smile. "You know how independent he is."

"Too bad." Olivia's voice hardened. "His independence almost got him killed."

Silence settled around them. Xander's breathing slowed first, then Tammy's. Olivia stared into the darkness, sleep eluding her despite the exhaustion weighing on her limbs. The choices before her waged war in her mind. Continue the investigation and risk more violence. Abandon it and leave Wally's attacker free to strike again. Report everything to the police and lose control of the investigation. None of the options offered safety. None guaranteed answers.

Olivia dozed fitfully, dreams filled with dark tunnels and grasping hands.

Chapter 14

Morning arrived with a flash of daylight as the back door opened, waking Tammy. Mrs. T swept in, a white bakery box in hand, filling the room with the warm delights of cinnamon and sugar.

"Look what I've got!" Mrs. Temperance waved a newspaper with her free hand. Her eyes twinkled despite the creases in her blouse from sleeping upright all night.

Tammy pushed herself up from the floor, her hair rumpled. "You went out alone?"

"To Sweet Crumbs, dear. It's next door." Mrs. T set the box on the table. "Should I not have gone?"

"After what happened with Wally, we need to be careful," said Tammy.

"I assumed he was okay, or you would have woken me," said Mrs. T. "Is he hurt?"

"Yes," said Olivia. "But we need to fetch him from the hospital."

"We can eat the pastries and read the newspaper on the way," said Mrs. T, who was much chirpier than everyone else after sleeping through everything.

Xander reached for the newspaper. "New clues?"

"Let's find out together," Mrs. T said.

"Everyone in the car," said Tammy.

Lockie leaped onto the back seat, surveying the scene from above.

Tammy pulled away from the curb. *What new twist would today bring?*

From the passenger seat, Mrs. T read the headline: "Mystery Skeleton Found in Prohibition-Era Tunnel Under Swinging Spoon Diner." She scanned the article. "Authorities confirmed the unidentified body was female and died at least fifty years ago!"

"Wow," Tammy murmured, her grip tightening on the steering wheel. She remembered the dank, moldy smell, the endless dark passages, and the pile of bones.

"It fits our timeline," Mrs. Temperance said.

The image of Wally, injured and alone in a hospital bed overwhelmed Tammy. She should be thinking about Wally, not the skeleton. The thought of him attacked while pursuing their investigation didn't sit right with her.

"I hope Wally's all right." Tammy acknowledged the road sign—still ten minutes from the hospital. Ten minutes of not knowing.

Olivia nodded, her fingers stroking Lockie's fur. "Me too. But Wally's tough."

"He shouldn't have been alone," Tammy said, guilt gnawing at her stomach. "We should have gone with him to the library." Who would attack an ex-sheriff? And over what—old newspaper articles?

She pressed the accelerator hard, urgency fueling her speed. The needle crept past the speed limit. Her usual caution warred with her need to reach Wally now.

The hospital loomed ahead, sterile and imposing. Tammy pulled into the parking lot and killed the engine.

Olivia lifted Lockie and placed him on the seat.

"Stay here Lockie, while we go get Wally," she said.

They hurried inside. The receptionist directed them to Wally's room with a sympathetic smile. Tammy's mouth ran dry.

The door swung open with a whoosh. Wally sat propped against pillows, his familiar weathered face pale but alert. A white bandage wrapped around his head, stark against his gray hair, with a small spot of red seeping through behind his ear—evidence of violence against someone she cared for.

His face broke into a crooked smile. "About time you all got here. I'm ready to blow this popsicle stand."

Relief flooded through Tammy, nearly buckling her knees. She steadied herself against the doorframe.

"Take it easy, Wally," said Olivia. "You need to recover."

Wally waved a dismissive hand. "I'm fine. A bump on the head is all. I've survived worse."

"Don't you ever scare us like that again!" Mrs. Temperance admonished.

"Do we need to rethink this investigation?" Tammy asked. "This isn't worth someone getting hurt."

Olivia's head snapped toward her. "You don't mean that."

"I do." Tammy crossed her arms. "We're not trained for this. We're a bookstore owner, a retired teacher, a writer, and—"

"An ex-sheriff," Wally interrupted. "Who's telling you we need to keep going."

Xander cleaned his glasses. "Someone was willing to hurt Wally. They might come after one of us next."

"I've been thinking about that. All night," said Olivia.

"No one signed up for violence," Mrs. Temperance said. "But someone resorted to it, which means we're close to something important."

"Or dangerous," Tammy countered.

"Life is dangerous," Wally said. "And someone already tried to silence us. Running away now won't make us any safer."

Tammy met his eyes. "You don't know that." Doubt slipped into her voice before she could stop it.

Wally's eyes didn't waver, and something about the strength in his look made her swallow hard.

"I know backing down from bullies only encourages them," he said. "And I know whoever's buried under the diner deserves justice, just as I deserve to know who attacked me and why."

The resolve in his voice was unmistakable. One by one, they nodded, though some were slower than others, as if wrestling with doubt.

Wally grimaced as he shifted against the pillows. His expression darkened, mouth settling into a thin line. "Someone wanted me out of the way, and they almost succeeded."

Tammy moved closer to the bed, her writer's imagination conjuring shadowy figures lurking in the library stacks, waiting for Wally to be alone.

Xander stepped forward. "What happened?"

"I discovered there was no bank heist in Stonefield, ever! Someone made a fake newspaper article to throw us off the scent. Or set a trap."

Olivia gasped. "A trap. By who?"

"Someone desperate to hinder this investigation," Wally said. "Someone who doesn't want us digging up the past." His jaw clenched. "They caught me by surprise among the microfilm machines. Knocked me out cold. By the time I came to, they were long gone. And they'd taken my phone."

A chill crept along Tammy's spine. "One of the descendants. We ruffled feathers with our questions."

Wally nodded. "That's my guess. They wanted to scare us off, keep their family secrets buried." The lines of his face tightened, determination clear. "Well, it's going to take more than a knock to the head to stop me."

Olivia reached out and squeezed his hand. "We won't let them get away with this, no matter what they throw at us."

Around the room, heads dipped. No one spoke. Her chest tightened. Someone had hurt Wally to protect a lie. She wouldn't let them get away with it.

"Let's get you home so we can figure this out," Tammy suggested.

"Sounds like a plan." Wally swung his legs over the side of the bed. He paused before attempting to stand. She moved closer, not offering direct help but staying close enough to catch him if he stumbled.

With the team's subtle assistance, he stood and gathered his belongings. The nurse arrived with discharge papers and instructions for care. He would need watching; concussions are unpredictable.

"I'll fetch Wally's car from the library," Olivia said, already heading for the door. "I'll meet you in the parking lot."

Wally signed the papers, his usual neat script wobbled. Tammy met Mrs. Temperance's gaze and saw the same unease reflected in her eyes. They'd need to ensure he actually rested, regardless of his protests.

Once they stepped into the morning light, Tammy shifted more of Wally's weight onto herself. He'd never admit it, but he needed the help. Olivia was already waiting outside, idling Wally's car beside Tammy's.

"Let's put our phones on speaker so we can all talk while we drive," suggested Xander.

"Mine's gone, remember?" Wally said with a grimace.

What did the attacker want with Wally's phone?

"We'll share," Olivia said, holding up her device. "We'll get you a new one a.s.a.p."

The others agreed and organized their calls before splitting into the cars—Wally, Olivia, and Xander in Wally's car, Mrs. Temperance, Lockie, and Tammy in hers. Moments later, both vehicles pulled onto the road toward Willowcroft, their occupants deep in conversation via speakerphone.

"None of the descendants we met knew anything," said Olivia.

"The Walshes were acting suspicious, though," said Tammy. "Maybe he knew more than he let on."

"What about the hang ups?" asked Xander.

"We should make a list of those who might be in the area," said Wally.

Tammy frowned at the phone. Wally should be resting, not analyzing suspects. But arguing would only make him more determined.

"Could they have flown in from Florida?" asked Mrs. T.

"There's been enough time to fly in from anywhere in the country," said Tammy.

"Would they come all this way to commit murder?" asked Mrs. T.

"If they wanted the secret to stay buried, then yes," said Wally.

The lush greenery of the surrounding countryside filled their view as they continued to discuss possibilities.

"Regardless," Mrs. Temperance said, "we'll find them."

"Agreed," Tammy said. "We will find out how Max got in and out of the bank, where he hid the money, and who attacked Wally." She left unsaid what she wanted to do when they found the attacker.

The conversation continued until the fields gave way to familiar town streets. A few minutes later, Tammy pulled into the back entrance of the bookstore. As soon as she shifted into park, everyone piled out of the vehicles and converged on Wally. His pallor had worsened during the drive.

"Let me help you," Olivia said, taking his arm.

Wally waved them off. "I'm fine, I'm fine," he insisted, but the tightness around his mouth betrayed him. He gritted his teeth as he pushed himself to his feet. "I want to help with the investigation."

Tammy opened the door for him. "Stubborn old man."

Mrs. Temperance tutted as she came around to his side. "At least let us get you settled inside. I'll put the kettle on. A cup of sweet tea will do you good."

Wally didn't argue, which told Tammy more about his condition than any medical report. She stayed close, ready to grab his arm if he wobbled, though she knew better than to offer outright. He'd refuse on principle.

Inside, Lockie wound around his ankles, letting out an insistent meow that rose in pitch like a question, then a scolding. The cat glanced at Wally, then Tammy, as if demanding she do something about this human's foolishness.

"Yes, Lockie," she murmured. "I'm on it."

Once Wally was seated at the table in the back room with a steaming mug of Mrs. Temperance's sweet tea, he exhaled deeply. Some of the tension in his shoulders eased. Tammy spied the slight tremor in his hands as he lifted the mug, the effort it took to appear normal.

"I know you all want me to rest," he said, meeting each of their concerned faces, "but they win if we slow down. And I'm not giving them a win."

Olivia nodded. "We need to go over all the descendants. One of them must be involved."

Tammy bit back her objection. Wally needed rest, but he also needed purpose. They'd compromise. "We'll work on the case," she said, "but you're staying in that chair. No field trips, no heavy lifting—mental or physical. Deal?"

Wally's mouth quirked into a half-smile. "Deal."

Chapter 15

Olivia scanned the morning newspaper article again, focusing on the skeleton being female. "I'm going to search for female bank employees."

"Great idea," Mrs. T said.

Olivia opened her laptop. "I'll start with Willowcroft's 1950 Census."

"Let me see what I can find online," Xander offered, pulling out his laptop and getting to work.

Tammy moved back and forth between Olivia and Xander, waiting to see who would discover something first. Lockie jumped onto a nearby chair, honing in on the unofficial contest.

"Got it." Olivia's databases won this round. "There was only one female employee at the bank."

"Banking was not an appropriate career path for a woman back then," said Mrs. T.

"Cathy Robinson," was all Olivia said.

Everyone glared at her.

"As in Mary Collins's best friend?" clarified Tammy.

"The age stated fits with what Cathy and Mary would have been in 1950."

"What was her role?" Tammy asked as she moved behind Olivia to read her screen. "Housekeeper."

"Typical," said Mrs. T, giving a curt nod in the air.

"She had access to the bank," Wally said. "Was she the inside man? No one pays any attention to the janitor."

Mrs. T tutted.

"What do we know about Cathy?" Tammy asked.

"She was alive after Mary died because we have her statement," said Xander as he delved into the files from Mary's case. "Cathy confirmed Mary was in a romantic relationship with Victor Walsh, describing him as attentive and fond of her. She recalled him bringing Mary flowers and taking her to the movies, emphasizing they appeared happy with no signs of tension or jealousy.

"When asked if she knew anyone who might have harmed Mary, Cathy insisted Mary was well-liked and didn't mention any potential threats. She also dismissed robbery as a motive, stating Mary lived simply and had nothing of value to steal.

"However, the interviewing officer noted that while Cathy was cooperative, she seemed hesitant, pausing before some of her responses."

"Now I remember," said Tammy. "We questioned whether she was nervous or withholding information."

"What happened to her afterward?" Wally asked.

Olivia's fingers had been dancing over the keyboard throughout the discussion. "Nothing. I can't find a marriage or death certificate."

"Is she still alive?" asked Xander.

"Or the skeleton in the tunnels," said Tammy, sombering the mood.

"What about her family?" asked Mrs. T.

"The census records show her living with her parents and younger brother in town."

"Younger brother as in Mrs. Robinson the piano teacher's husband?" suggested Xander.

"Brilliant," said Wally, giving Xander a proud pat on the back.

"Mrs. Robinson's husband was James," said an animated Mrs. T.

Olivia searched her notes. "Yes. The younger brother was James."

"Mrs. Robinson was my piano teacher," said Xander. "She had old photos displayed everywhere. I could ask her about Cathy."

Tammy recalled the piano music from the tunnels. If Cathy was the skeleton, had she known she was underneath her house? Had she heard music in her last moments?

"Great idea," Wally encouraged Xander. "Mrs. Temperance, would you like to join him? You must know Mrs. Robinson. She might open up more with you there."

Mrs. T grabbed her handbag and shawl. "Of course. Come along, Xander. Let's walk over now."

Xander's sneakers scuffed against the sidewalk as he followed Mrs. Temperance toward the familiar yellow Victorian. The same house he had visited dozens of times for piano lessons, back when his dad thought music might help him be more "well-rounded." Whatever that meant.

Mrs. Temperance reached for the brass knocker, and Xander hung back, shifting his weight from foot to foot. Social calls weren't his jam. He never knew where to stand or what to do with his hands. The door creaked open, revealing Mrs. Robinson, looking exactly as she had during his lessons.

"Why, Hazel, Xander!" Her warm greeting made his shoulders relax. At least Mrs. Robinson never treated him like a social misfire.

The living room hadn't changed either. The same floral-patterned couch that was soft and formal, the same smell of furniture polish. Xander perched on the edge of the couch, trying not to fidget as Mrs. Temperance launched straight into detective mode.

His attention sharpened at the mention of Cathy.

"Cathy was my late husband's sister." Mrs. Robinson's words were slow and careful, like testing the ice before stepping onto a frozen lake. "But I'm afraid I can't help you much. She left Willowcroft long ago and never returned."

Xander leaned forward. "Why did she leave?" The question tumbled out, earning a quick glance from Mrs. Temperance.

Something flickered across Mrs. Robinson's face as she turned toward the mantelpiece. Xander followed her gaze to an old photograph.

"She left a note one day, saying goodbye and that she was going to chase her dreams of being a city girl. The family thought she didn't want to be reminded of her small-town roots. After her best friend Mary died, there was nothing left for her here in Willowcroft."

People didn't vanish without a trace, not even back then. There were always digital breadcrumbs. Or in this case, paper ones.

"James said Cathy and Mary were inseparable growing up, sharing everything, including their dreams of leaving Willowcroft."

"And she never contacted her family again?" Mrs. T asked.

Mrs. Robinson's hand smoothed her skirt. "James was only eight when she left. Every birthday, he'd blow out his candles and wish for her to come home. Every Christmas, he'd set aside a present for her."

She paused, swallowing hard. "For years, he'd rush to the door whenever the bell rang, convinced it might be Cathy. Even as a grown man, he'd hesitate before answering the phone, holding his breath with this... this terrible hope. He kept her bedroom exactly as it was when she left. 'Just in case,' he'd say."

A young woman disappearing without a trace, leaving her family behind—it was like something out of one of his true crime podcasts. But this wasn't a story. Mrs. Robinson looked wrecked.

"That must have been awful for James," Xander said, surprising himself with the empathy in his voice. "To lose his sister when he was a kid."

Mrs. Robinson nodded, her fingers fiddling with a lace thing on the arm of her chair. "It wasn't just losing Cathy; it was the not knowing. Some nights I'd find him sitting at the kitchen table at three in the morning, staring at old photographs, wondering if she was alive or dead, happy or suffering. 'Does she ever think of us?' he'd ask me. Questions without answers."

Her face pinched as she grabbed a framed photo from the side table.

"This was taken the summer before she left."

The photo showed a young woman with wild hair laughing, her arm wrapped around a little dude's shoulders. They totally looked alike.

The bookcase swung open with a thud against the wall.

Tammy lifted her head from the scattered papers as Xander burst through, Mrs. Temperance on his heels.

"We've got it!" he exclaimed. "Cathy disappeared right after Mary's murder."

Xander and Mrs. Temperance explained what they had learned from Mrs. Robinson.

"Don't you see?" Olivia said. "Cathy must have been involved in the bank robbery with Max."

Mrs. Temperance raised her hand. "Let's take this one step at a time. *If Cathy was involved in the heist, it might explain why she ended up dead in the tunnel. But it's not proof.*"

Tammy stretched and yawned. "My brain is fried. I think it's time for a little creative lollygagging."

They stared at her, blank and unblinking.

It was what I was doing when the idea for the stolen manuscript book took hold.

"Creative lollygagging?" Xander asked. "Are you making stuff up?"

Tammy laughed. "It's something writers do to stimulate creativity when they're stuck. We indulge in mindless activities to let our minds wander and make unexpected connections."

"I'm intrigued," said Olivia. "What do you have in mind?"

Tammy turned to Xander. "Can you put all the photos we have into a slideshow? Including everything on Mary Collins?"

"Sure thing," Xander replied with enthusiasm, pulling out his laptop and getting to work.

"Olivia," Tammy continued, "did I see popcorn in one of your cupboards the other day?"

"Why, yes you did," Olivia answered with a grin.

"Great!" Mrs. T interjected, catching on. "I'll make a pot of hot cocoa."

Tammy clapped her hands. "Perfect. Let's snack and sip while we watch a movie of sorts and see if something new jumps out at us now that we have a few more pieces in the puzzle. Creative lollygagging at its finest!"

The team buzzed around the bookstore, setting up the projector, gathering refreshments, and rearranging chairs into a makeshift theater. Lockie, confused by the sudden flurry of activity, darted between their legs, trying to keep up.

Soon, buttery deliciousness scented the air and the projector screen lit the room.

"Now let's relax, nourish our brains, and see what happens," Tammy said. With calm restored, Lockie relaxed and purred nearby.

Xander started the slideshow, and one by one, the photos from their investigation crossed the screen in larger-than-life size. They watched in silence, munching on popcorn and sipping their cocoa, allowing their minds to wander.

When the photos from Mary Collins' file popped up, a sad sigh spread across the room. The images showed various aspects of her life—happy moments, candid shots, and the gruesome scene of her murder.

"Wait, go back," Olivia said, jumping forward in her chair. "That's Mary. Victor has his hand around her waist, but there's a third person. The woman's holding Mary's hand, and they are smiling at each other, not at Victor or the camera."

Xander approached the screen. "Mrs. T, do you think it's Cathy?"

Mrs. Temperance leaned forward and squinted at the image. "Yes, but we already know Mary and Cathy were friends."

"Let's keep going and see if anything else jumps out."

The team continued pouring over the photos, searching for clues.

"Wait," Xander said. "I'm going back one."

An old black-and-white photo of three men in a field appeared. They'd confirmed the men were the names from the notebook: Clark Michaels, Samuel Grey, and Victor Walsh.

"I think I recognize the fence in the background," Wally said, squinting. "Isn't that like the one by your cottage, Tammy?"

Tammy peered at the image projected on the wall. "I think you're right! That's my side fence. Which means this photo was taken in the field next door."

How did I miss that?

"Fascinating," murmured Mrs. Temperance. "Yet another connection back to your cottage. It seems to be the center of everything."

Lockie, startled by the sudden exclamations, leapt off Mrs. Temperance's lap and hid under a chair.

"Sorry, Lockie!" Tammy said. "We're excited because this shows the three men from the notebook meeting by my cottage, where Mary died."

"What were they discussing?" Olivia asked. "They're acting proud of themselves."

Tammy clapped her hands. "So, creative lollygagging is not such a bad idea."

Wally chuckled. "It's the most relaxing detective work I've ever done."

Tammy nodded as she studied the photo. *Nathan was convinced the money was at the cottage. Now, here were three people from his notebook captured in a photo near the same place.*

"I think it's time we explored those fields near my cottage. There might be something there tying all of this together."

Wally's wince was audible as he shifted in his chair. Mrs. Temperance gave him a concerned glance. "Perhaps we should call it a night and let Wally rest."

"No, no, I'm all right," Wally protested. "We're so close; I can feel it. Let's keep following this trail while it's fresh."

Tammy gave Wally an appreciative smile. His dedication, despite being injured, inspired her.

"It's too late to go exploring today anyway. First thing tomorrow, though," Tammy said. "I'll make us a hearty breakfast to fuel our expedition. The answers could be right under our noses."

Chapter 16

Xander was pacing around his room, totally annoyed as he re-read the weird note his parents got that morning:

Stay out of matters that don't concern you. This is your only warning.

His parents were freaking out about his safety and kept arguing over whether they'd allow him to continue with the treasure hunt.

"Absolutely not," said Xander's mom, crossing her arms and pacing like crazy. "He's a teenager. This is getting too dangerous."

"Wally will protect him," suggested his dad. Park Ranger Dan to the rescue.

But Xander, eavesdropping from his room, was already boiling with frustration. This adventure, even with all the danger, had been the best summer ever. There was no way he was going to miss out now when they were so close to cracking the mystery.

"Fine," he grumbled, grabbing the cryptic notebook Nathan had doodled in. "If I can't go with them, I'll solve it from here."

He snatched a pencil and started scribbling like mad, determined to crack the next code in Max's dementia ramblings.

He'd keep searching, with or without his parents' approval.

The acrid smell of almost-burnt bacon made Tammy's nose twitch. There was a fine line between crispy and charred—rather like the line between cautiously optimistic and foolishly naive about the investigation. Mother would have something cutting to say about both her cooking skills and her judgment.

The knock at the door scattered her thoughts. Her makeshift detective team huddled on her porch, their faces wearing expressions that usually preceded bad news in chapter three of a mystery novel.

They thrust forward envelopes, each bearing the same aggressive handwriting screaming anger.

Uh oh.

"We found one on your car too," Olivia said, extending another envelope like it might bite.

"What do they say?"

"Leave the money alone or there will be consequences," read Olivia.

"Stay away from the bank heist," said Wally.

"Back off now, or you'll regret it," said Mrs. T.

Tammy opened hers. "Keep your nose out of it."

Too late.

She herded them inside.

Mrs. Temperance collapsed into a chair, her fuchsia shawl a defiant splash of color against the mounting tension. The way she smoothed her note against the table reminded Tammy of her own nervous habit of straightening manuscript pages.

"It's clear someone wants to deter us from pursuing this further," said Mrs. T.

And yet here we all are, amateur sleuths refusing to back off.

Wally lowered himself into a chair, bracing one hand on the table as he eased down. "We've come too far to stop now."

If this were one of my books, the threatening notes would be a sure sign we're getting close.

Mrs. Temperance pursed her lips. "I received a call from Xander's parents this morning. They forbade him from leaving the house after getting one of these notes."

"Xander must be so frustrated," sighed Olivia.

"We must press on," said Mrs. T.

"Let's eat so we can explore," said Tammy, who served everyone crispy bacon, one step below cremation.

There was only one topic of conversation.

"Maybe they were celebrating after hiding the stolen money," suggested Olivia between bites of toast. "Or it's a clue to where Max stashed it."

"Both possibilities are worth considering," said Wally, rubbing his temple as if trying to dispel a persistent ache. "We should study the photo again once we're out in the fields."

Tammy finished her coffee. "Let's get ready."

Lockie meowed in agreement, jumping onto the windowsill to observe their progress as they prepared to leave the cozy refuge of the little blue cottage.

Honeysuckle perfume drifted on the breeze as they stepped outside—sweet and innocent, at total odds with the threatening notes on her kitchen table. *Like the opening of a cozy mystery right before everything goes wrong.* She led them through her side gate to their next adventure as sheep grazed in the distance.

Tammy pulled out the old photograph. Her writer's eye matched angles and shadows, the past overlaying the present.

"Based on the angle, I'd say they were standing right about... there." She pointed to a small rise.

"Where's Lockie?" asked Mrs. Temperance, searching. A rustle came from the tall grass, and Lockie emerged, tail twitching. The cat was drawn to a particular spot, sniffing and pawing at the earth as if urging them to investigate.

"Lockie found something," Olivia said.

Trust the cat—isn't that what all the great mystery writers say?

Drawing closer, Tammy spotted an old ring of stones, now overgrown with vines and weeds.

"This must be it," she said. The team gathered around.

Wally's trowel attacked the vegetation with purpose. He paused after hacking through one stubborn root, then straightened with a grunt before diving back into the task. Each hack brought them closer to... what? *Please don't let this be another dead end or body.*

Wally gave a triumphant shout as the solid thunk of metal against wood sounded. They brushed away the last of the debris to reveal a weathered wooden hatch. Tammy's breath caught in her throat.

"Do you think...?" Olivia whispered.

Wally reached for the rusted metal ring embedded in the wood, planting his feet to get leverage. Seeing him square his shoulders for the effort, Tammy recalled the pale face she'd seen at the hospital, the way his signature had wobbled.

No. Sudden, jarring strain is the last thing his head needs. *He'll hurt himself.* Her protective instincts surged as she nudged him aside.

He gave her a sharp look, maybe halfway between annoyance at being sidelined and reluctant understanding, but he moved aside.

Tammy gripped the pitted metal ring. Cold and rough beneath her fingers, flakes of rust clung to her skin. She braced herself, planting her feet. Pulling steadily at first, the hatch resisted, fused by time and neglect.

She took a deeper breath, put her full weight into a hard heave, her shoulder muscles bunched. For a tense second, nothing; then a gut-wrenching screech set Tammy's teeth on edge, and it yielded upward. The musty breath of the underground wafted from an earthen ramp descending into darkness.

"Is this the same tunnel as under the diner?" asked Tammy.

Mrs. Temperance peered into the shadows. "It would appear we've stumbled upon another entrance."

"But Stanton hasn't blocked off this one," said Wally.

"He probably doesn't know about it," said Olivia.

Adrenaline zinged through Tammy's system. She observed her friends, discovering her own thrill reflected in their faces. *We're doing this. We're actually doing this.*

Wally flicked on a flashlight. "Shall we?"

"Let's go." The words came out steadier than she expected. Lockie sniffed at the entrance with his ears pricked forward. *What clues are you picking up, little detective?*

Wally distributed lights and the cautionary words seemed pulled straight from every adventure novel she'd ever read. *Though those protagonists had better equipment than dollar store specials.*

"Lockie, you're with me." Tammy fastened a tiny light next to his flashing red beacon, grateful for his steady presence. The cat's alert posture suggested he sensed something.

Loose dirt crunched beneath her shoes as she kept one hand pressed against the earthen wall, its cool dampness grounding her in reality. This passage had a raw, primitive edge that the town square tunnel lacked, like stepping back through time itself.

Wally's beam danced ahead, carving a path through the gloom. "Imagine if this connects to the other tunnels," he mused. "Could be an entire network."

"Possible hideouts for bootleggers back in the day," Mrs. Temperance remarked.

The ramp ended at a room that seemed to breathe darkness, even under their combined lights. Water trickled down the walls like whispered scandals, and the decay-laden air caught in her throat. *Mother would have a field day with this—crawling through underground passages like some discount Indiana Jones.*

"Fascinating," breathed Mrs. T, peering into the gloom.

"Feels like we're walking into the mouth of some ancient beast," said Tammy.

"With luck, not a hungry one," Wally said.

Mrs. T wrapped her colorful shawl more tightly around her shoulders. "There's something in the air... like the walls remember."

"Let's not get carried away," Wally warned. "Danger may lurk in these depths."

"But think of all the mysteries we might uncover!" said Olivia.

Up ahead, Wally grunted.

The women crowded around to see what had stopped him. A large wooden door blocked their path. It might as well have had "PLOT TWIST" carved into its weathered surface. *Why does there always have to be a locked door?* Its wood splintered and warped from years of exposure to the damp. A rusted padlock hung from the latch.

"Meow."

"What is it, Lockie?"

Please don't let it be rats.

Lockie honed in on an opening in the wall.

Tammy knelt beside him. She gasped. "Look at this!" Nestled within the dusty recess sat a roll of yellowed paper.

As the group gathered around, Tammy unrolled the fragile item, revealing a crudely drawn map of what appeared to be their current tunnel system. She traced her fingers over the brittle parchment, the rough texture catching against her skin. The ink had faded but was discernible.

"Amazing," Mrs. T whispered, leaning in. "How did it survive down here for so long?"

It's not even damp.

"Convenient," mumbled Wally. "What we need, right when we need it."

Intricate symbols and markings hinted at chambers and passageways throughout the network.

"Is there an 'X' marking the spot?" Olivia asked.

CLANG!

THUMP!

The sounds hit like a physical blow, sending Tammy's heart into her throat.

No, no, no...

The entrance door had slammed shut.

Panic clawed at her chest, each breath shorter than the last.

This isn't how the story's supposed to go. It's way too early for another plot twist.

Lockie's fur bristled as he crouched low, releasing a guttural snarl that made Tammy's blood run cold. The sound confirmed her suspicion.

Someone had sealed them in.

Chapter 17

"Oh, fudgsicle." Mrs. T put a hand to her chest. "This reminds me of the old coal mine tour I took with my students in '82. We were underground for three hours."

A wave of claustrophobia washed over Tammy, and she had to suppress a shiver. "Who locked us in here?" Her voice quavered. "Was someone following us? Is this another trap?"

"Let's stay calm," Wally said. "We'll find another way out." His flashlight moved to the second door and highlighted his hand pressing on it. "If it's connected to the other tunnels, then there's an exit at the Swinging Spoon and potentially others."

Tammy bit her lip. "We need to get past that door."

"What does the map say?" Olivia asked. "Let's marinate on our options before we decide we're in a real pickle."

Tammy took a deep breath to calm her scattered thoughts so she could focus on the map.

Olivia, appearing frustratingly calm despite their predicament, jabbed a finger at the map in Tammy's hands. "The little blue cottage is marked."

Tammy followed Olivia's finger. So it was. By the cottage sat a small illustration of a door. "That must be the entrance we came through, and this is the big room we are standing in now."

"The tunnels lead off from the other side of that door." Olivia pointed her beam at the locked barrier.

"Our way out is forward through the tunnels?" Mrs. T asked.

"Whoever locked us in might be back any minute," said Wally.

"Hey, I recognize this symbol!" Olivia pointed at a small pestle-and-mortar sign on the map, identical to the one they'd found on the tunnel side of the entrance beneath the Swinging Spoon. "The map can take us there, and we'll come across the crime scene tape or the diner," said Olivia.

"There are symbols and markings all over this map," Wally said. "They could lead to hidden rooms and other passages."

"And exit points," said Mrs. T. "Let's trust the map."

"We've got to get through this door first," said Tammy.

Wally jiggled the lock. It held firm. He took a half step back and braced his shoulder. Tammy tensed, the telltale signs of strain she'd already seen. *He shouldn't...*

Olivia darted forward, stepping between him and the door. "Whoa there, Sheriff. Pretty sure brute force is our department today. Girl power in action."

Wally paused, looking from Olivia to the door, then back again. A hint of something—maybe relief disguised as chagrin—flickered in his eyes before he gave a curt nod and stepped back, crossing his arms.

Thank goodness. Well done, Liv.

"All right, partner," Tammy positioned herself beside Olivia. "On three?"

Olivia highlighted her face as if she were about to tell a ghost story by a campfire, her grin exaggerated and eerie. "Let's make this door toast."

Wally and Mrs. T held the four lights on the door. Tammy and Olivia planted their feet on the uneven earth, lined up their shoulders, and pushed together on Olivia's count. The wood groaned but held, jarring against their shoulders. Lockie let out an encouraging chirp from near Tammy's ankles.

"Again!" Olivia grunted.

They slammed into it once more. A satisfying crack escaped from the door as jagged splinters feathered outward.

"One more time!" she yelled, adrenaline masking the ache in her shoulder.

A final, synchronized, mighty shove sent tremors through the rotting wood. The middle splintered inward, creating an opening big enough to climb through.

Tammy rubbed her shoulder, her breath coming in quick gasps. "Okay. Step one accomplished." She exchanged a triumphant smile with Olivia before turning to Wally, who dipped his chin in acknowledgment. "Let's get back to the surface."

Tammy retrieved her flashlight from Wally and climbed through first. Behind her, the splintered edges of the wood caught on Mrs. T's shawl, tugging at the fringe. Tammy reached back to help, but Mrs. T gave a quick twist and slipped free, her nimble movements belied her age.

Wally and Olivia followed, with Lockie sniffing the opening before joining them in a single leap.

The space beyond revealed a passage framed with wooden beams. Tree roots pierced the walls like nature's skeleton.

If I wrote this scene, readers would expect something lurking in those shadows. A red herring, perhaps, or the first glimpse of the true villain.

Tammy shone her light forward. "Let's go." She forced her novelist's imagination back into its box.

"Watch for any markings or signs," Olivia said. "We might find a detour to the treasure chamber. Wouldn't that be a delicious discovery?"

Mrs. Temperance stepped over a protruding root. "These tunnels have been untouched for so long; the potential discoveries are endless."

They rounded a slight bend, and Wally raised a hand. Tammy stopped. He spotlighted a faint marking on the wall—an etched arrow, pointing deeper into the darkness.

"We're on the right track," Mrs. Temperance said.

"Let's follow it," Tammy said.

"Stay vigilant," Wally warned as they pressed on, following the trail of markings through the maze of tunnels.

Lockie stayed close to Tammy's legs as they walked. His ears stood at attention, and every few steps, he stopped, nose twitching as he sampled the air before padding forward again. His collar flickered red as he moved, creating dancing shadows on the tunnel walls.

At least Lockie would alert us if anyone tried to sneak up on us. The perfect sidekick for an amateur detective.

"Did you hear that?" Olivia whispered, freezing mid-step. Her beam scanned the shadows.

"Probably rats," Mrs. Temperance said.

"That doesn't simmer down my nerves one bit."

"How did all this get forgotten?" Tammy ran her hand along the cool stone wall, imagining the stories embedded in each crack and crevice.

"There was no need for it once Prohibition ended," said Wally.

"Michigan was the first state to repeal it. First in, first out," said Mrs. T. "We understood more than most the damage caused."

"Some of these tunnels seem older than the 1920s," said Olivia. "What else could they be for? The plot thickens like a good roux."

Lockie let out a soft growl. His tail flicked back and forth. Fur rose along his spine.

Tammy swept her flashlight over the crumbling stone walls. The tunnel forked into two paths. She paused, illuminating each option. To the left, the way sloped upward, likely back toward the surface. To the right, it disappeared deeper underground to parts unknown.

In my books, the right path would hold the secrets, but the left would be the safe choice. The heroine always chooses wrong the first time.

She consulted the map. "The pestle and mortar is on the left branch."

"Makes sense," said Mrs. T. "If we were above ground, turning left would take us into town."

The older woman wheezed in the damp air, and Tammy's stomach twisted. *What was she thinking, bringing a woman in her seventies underground?* And adding an injured ex-sheriff to the mix? *Reckless.*

As they turned the corner, Tammy spotted it: the yellow crime scene tape stretched across the tunnel, a grim reminder of what they'd discovered five days ago.

Chapter 18

Xander slouched over Nathan's notebook. His brain fired on all cylinders as he tried to crack the enigma of Max Cross's words sprawled across the pages before him.

He'd scrutinized every inch of these pages, tracing over each line multiple times, squinting for obscure patterns or ciphers that might spill the beans. He'd already read a ton of cryptography books from Olivia's store, convinced there was some complex message lurking in this mess of words, waiting to be cracked.

He'd tried everything: transposition ciphers, substitution ciphers, Caesar shifts, and Vigenère squares. Every so-called lead collapsed into nonsense. It was driving him nuts.

And then it hit him.

The same words kept repeating.

Mary.

Saw.

Blue cottage.

Fireplace.

Money.

He jumped in his seat. It wasn't some fancy code or old-school encryption at all. Max was telling the same story over and over, all scrambled up. Dementia had messed with his narrative, scattering bits and pieces across

Nathan's notes. But everything was there, hiding in plain sight. Xander just hadn't seen it.

Bias is a trip. If someone tells you it's coded, you believe it—even when the truth is staring you in the face. His stomach twisted. He'd been so focused on finding concealed meanings that he overlooked the obvious.

His gut turned.

He dropped back into the chair, notebook open in front of him, brain rearranging the sentences like a game of word Tetris.

A pattern emerged.

A story.

"Of course!" He ran a hand through his hair, pulse racing as the realization hit. "The money's not in the tunnels."

He had to tell the others—like, ASAP.

Xander hunched over his phone, sending another text to the team. Still nothing. A tight knot twisted in his stomach as he stared at the unanswered messages. They'd gone to search the field behind the little blue cottage hours ago. Why weren't they answering?

His leg bounced, and his fingers gripped the phone so hard his knuckles ached. It was time to face the obvious: Tammy, Olivia, Wally, and Mrs. Temperance were missing.

He pushed his glasses up his nose and muttered, "Come on, guys," firing off another round of messages. Nothing.

I might be their only hope.

Even though his parents had forbidden him from leaving because the anonymous threat freaked them out, he couldn't abandon his friends when they were possibly hurt... or worse.

Xander grabbed his backpack, shoving Nathan's notebook inside before creeping downstairs. His parents were in the study, backs turned. Perfect.

He slipped out the front door without a sound.

Heat pressed against him as he hurried along the sidewalk toward the edge of town, sweat sticking his T-shirt to his back. The air was heavy and humid, matching the anxiety churning inside him. What if something happened to them in those tunnels?

When the little blue cottage came into view, he broke into a jog. He accessed the digital murder board on his phone and zoomed in on the image that had led them there. He scanned the field ahead.

There.

He hurried toward a patch of disturbed dirt.

Something was off. A large tree branch had been dragged over what appeared to be a hatch. The placement wasn't natural. If it opened from below, there'd be no way to push it free from inside.

Were they trapped?

"Tammy? Olivia? Wally?" His voice cracked as he called out.

Nothing.

With his heart pounding, he forced the branch aside, muscles straining with the effort, then wrenched the hatch open.

Cool, damp air rushed out to meet him. His fingers tightened around his phone.

This is a terrible idea.

He stepped inside anyway.

Darkness swallowed him. His breath came fast and sharp. He lifted his phone, flicking on the flashlight. Jagged dirt walls and packed earth beneath his feet came into view. He shivered. Last time they were here, they'd found human bones.

Now, he was alone.

"Guys, please be okay." He pressed deeper into the tunnels, light arching side to side, trying to listen past the hammering of his own heartbeat.

Where were they?

His mind raced through every possibility: Olivia, always leaping ahead, led by her curiosity and getting herself in trouble. Tammy, puzzle-solving at a mile a minute. Wally, the protector. Mrs. T, always sharp, always ahead of the game.

If something had happened to them—

No. Not thinking like that.

The tunnel twisted ahead. His beam caught a flash of color. Xander stopped short.

A scrap of yarn.

Purple. Mrs. T's shawl?

His hands clenched. They'd been through here. He was close.

As he stepped forward, his light landed on a dark shape on the ground.

His breath caught.

Not a body.

A pile of discarded clothes and belongings.

He gave a sharp exhale, tension rolling off his shoulders.

Then—voices.

He froze.

He flicked off the flashlight, pressing himself against the tunnel wall, breath shallow.

The voices grew clearer. Tammy's excited chatter. Olivia's calm, measured tone. Wally's gruff interjections.

They were okay.

He peeked around the bend and spotted them in a pool of light, talking to several deputies. Relief nearly buckled his knees.

Lockie paced at the edge of the group, tail flicking. He paused—glanced at Xander—but didn't give him away, instead trotting back to Tammy's side like nothing was amiss.

Xander managed a small smile. They were safe.

Yeah... but someone's still watching me.

The team walked into the brightly lit chamber. Two deputies whirled around, their hands hovering over their holstered weapons.

Wally thrust his hands up. "Whoa, easy there! We're on your side."

A muscular woman with a severe blonde bun stepped forward. "Where did you all come from?"

Tammy pointed behind them. "The tunnel back there. Someone trapped us inside."

The deputy's radio crackled at her hip. Yellow tape stretched across the chamber, marking the path from the Swinging Spoon entrance to the body.

"We have information about your investigation," Wally said. "Is Stanton around?"

Mrs. T leaned close to Wally. "Who is this deputy?"

"Must be new," he muttered in reply before taking a step forward. "Sorry to surprise you. We're investigating a series of events tied to an old bank robbery. We believe this tunnel system is connected, and—"

"Connected to what?" the officer interrupted, clearly not buying their story.

"Connected to the murder of Mary Collins and the disappearance of Cathy Robinson," Tammy interjected, her voice strong despite her fear. "We think Max Cross hid the stolen money down here, and there's a chance the skeleton is Cathy."

"And whoever locked us in might not have gone far," said Mrs. T.

The deputy's frown deepened. She barked orders into her radio for backup, then turned to the forensic techs working nearby. "Wrap it up. We need to sweep these tunnels."

She turned to the team. "Nobody moves until backup arrives."

The team huddled closer as the officers organized themselves. Olivia adjusted her glasses. "Do you really think whoever locked us in is lurking around?"

Wally's knuckles went white. "Not if he knows what's good for him."

Mrs. T smoothed her shawl, pulling at a loose thread. "Let's not jump to conclusions. Perhaps it was a misunderstanding."

Tammy scooped up Lockie protectively. "Be careful," she told the officers as they went deeper in the tunnel.

After a few tense minutes, Lockie hissed, his fur standing on end. A beam swung to reveal a figure crouched behind a rocky outcrop.

"Sheriff's Department! Put your hands up!" shouted the officer.

"Who are you? What are you doing here?" demanded the female officer.

"Xander!" Tammy exclaimed, rushing over to him. "What are you doing here? You were supposed to be safe at home with your parents."

Lockie rubbed against his legs, purring.

"Lockie would never have bristled at Xander," said Tammy. "Someone else is here."

Two more deputies arrived. After being briefed, they set about scouring the tunnels while the team waited anxiously.

Tammy's heart raced as she strained to hear anything indicating they'd found the culprit. But several minutes passed with no word from the searching officers. The tunnels were eerily silent, apart from the occasional scurry of rats in the distance that she was trying to ignore.

"Stop right there!" an officer commanded. Lights converged on a single point.

A figure stumbled from behind a debris pile. The officers secured him.

"We've found our troublemaker," Olivia said.

Xander turned to his friends. "I knew someone was watching me."

Tammy squinted at the stranger's face, searching for any hint of recognition. Nothing. "Anyone know him?"

Heads shook around her.

Mrs. T's purple shawl rustled as she straightened. "Start talking."

The officer's stance tightened. "These tunnels are restricted. They're part of an active investigation."

The man's mouth twisted. "My ancestors built these tunnels. I've got rights." He squared his shoulders. "Name's Andrew Walsh. I'm exploring my heritage."

Mrs. T's breath hitched. "Walsh? Peter Walsh's son?"

"Dad handed over those documents without a clue." Andrew smirked. "That map's been in my family for generations. Grandpa Victor had the map when the heist happened. Figured you amateur sleuths could do the legwork."

"You planted the map." Mrs. T's knuckles whitened around her shawl. "Trapped us."

"Smart lady." Andrew winked. "Once you found the cash, it would've been mine. Simple."

Wally lunged forward. "Simple? You cracked my skull!" His bandage had seeped red again.

"And those threatening letters," Olivia added.

Andrew's hands shot up. "The map and the lock-in? Yeah, that was me. But I never touched anyone or sent any notes."

Tammy stiffened. Wait—what? If Andrew hadn't sent those threats or attacked Wally, then who had?

She opened her mouth, then closed it again. The others focused on Andrew, but someone had to send the letters. And Wally... he could have been killed.

She swallowed hard. "If you didn't send them, then someone else did." The sentence landed heavily in the confined space, sharp against the silence.

Andrew said nothing. His smirk had faded.

Tammy glanced at Wally's bandage, at the dark red seeping through. He shifted his weight, jaw tight. Whoever had attacked him hadn't done it for fun. That wasn't a warning—that was intent.

And they still didn't know who.

Andrew's gaze fixed on her. "I knew it was only a matter of time before you uncovered the tunnel entrance on your land."

Heat crept up Tammy's neck as her fellow team members glared at her. "The cottage sale included those fields."

"Your land, your tunnels," Wally muttered.

"Enough." The officer yanked Andrew away. "We'll take it from here."

"I need to tell you something important," Xander said. "I cracked Nathan's notebook." He took a deep breath. "The money's not in the tunnels."

Chapter 19

"But it's close by..." Xander paused, seemingly unsure if he should reveal this information yet.

"Come on, spit it out!" Wally urged.

"Where's the loot?" Olivia asked.

"Don't keep us in suspense!" Tammy said. She was going to strangle him if he didn't spit it out.

"Not here."

"No one asked us to stay, so let's go to the bookstore and talk there," said Olivia.

"No," said Xander. "We need to go to Tammy's."

His suggestion was met with silence. Tammy peered around, noting the confusion on everyone's faces as she tried to understand the connection.

"My place? Why?" she asked.

Xander pushed his glasses up the bridge of his nose. "Based on what's in the notebook, the money has to be at the little blue cottage. Max mentioned Mary all the time—but never once said anything about the tunnels. That's what tipped me off."

Tammy frowned. "You think he was talking about the cottage, not the tunnels?"

Xander nodded. "I went back through the notebook. Every phrase is two or three words—nonsense on its own. But when I listed the most common ones and started grouping them, a pattern emerged. He kept circling the same ideas over and over."

He flipped to a page, pointing at his scribbled notes in the margins.

"'Mary... saw... blue cottage... fireplace... money.' That's the loop. No matter how many times he spiraled out, he always came back to those."

He tapped the word *saw*. "Cutting tools weren't part of the story, so it hit me—he wasn't talking about an object. He *saw* something. He *witnessed* it. That's when it all clicked."

"Nathan thought the money was in the fireplace," said Tammy. "That's why he broke in."

"Yeah," Xander said. "But he didn't know what we know. Max only hid *himself* in the fireplace after the murder. The weapon was there. Not the money."

Mrs. Temperance tapped a finger against her lip. "So Max saw the money. At the cottage."

"And that's where he left it," Xander said. "His mind might have gone, but it never let go of that."

Tammy's jaw dropped as the actual revelation hit her.

"The boy's cracked it," said Wally. "Let's follow it through. Olivia, you're the only one with a car left in town. You're driving."

Tammy climbed the stairs leading out from the tunnel exit beneath the Swinging Spoon. Yellow tape still crisscrossed the diner's entrance, marking it as an active crime scene. She followed the others through the back exit and around to Olivia's back door, where her car was parked.

Tammy pictured her cozy home, with its creaky floorboards and faded wallpaper. Where could the money be?

"The attic!" Tammy said. "When I first moved into the cottage, the letter that sparked this investigation was in the attic."

"Maybe Mary stashed everything she was hiding there," said Xander.

"How did two law enforcement searches miss it?" asked Mrs. T.

"I bet they didn't lift the floorboards and that's where the letter was," said Tammy.

Her mind reeled back to the day she had stumbled upon the cryptic note in the attic. What more was there to find?

Tammy's thoughts blurted out, "The letter had no context. We assumed the recipient, Mary, knew something about the sender, Max. But we may have had it backward this whole time. Max knew something about Mary."

The car hadn't even stopped when Tammy flung open her door, her heart quickening with urgency. Her desperation mirrored the faces around her. Wally vaulted from the backseat. Mrs. T moved quicker than Tammy had ever seen, and Lockie darted past Tammy's legs, his tail at attention.

Tammy rushed toward the cottage, her breath catching in her throat as she pushed through the door. She headed straight for the narrow attic staircase, the others close behind.

"Where should we start?" asked Olivia.

"Let's check under the floorboards first," suggested Wally.

The group spread out across the attic. Tammy's knees pressed into the rough wooden planks, wincing at the sting of splinters through her jeans. Her fingertips tingled as they drifted over each board, testing, searching. The hollow tap-tap-tap from the others matched her quickening pulse.

Was it here? Tammy's mouth went dry. She imagined Mary Collins sneaking up here, lifting a plank and concealing her secrets.

Tammy's fingernails caught the edge of the floorboard where she'd found the letter. She wedged her fingers beneath the wood.

The board surrendered with a groan. Dust exploded upward, tickling her nose and coating her hands. Decayed leaves scattered across the floor like confetti.

Xander aimed his flashlight into the opening. "There's something in there!"

Tammy froze.

Neat stacks of paper.

No—money.

The bills sat in perfect bundles, untouched for decades.

Faded green ink, the smaller size of old currency.

Were they real?

Her fingertips brushed the topmost bill. Cool. Crisp. Real.

"It's the money!" Olivia's exclamation pierced Tammy's stupor.

Tammy blinked, struggling to reconnect with reality. The cash beneath her fingers represented more than currency. Their amateur sleuthing wasn't a delusion or a waste of time.

"This is it." Xander's whisper carried the same awe rising in Tammy's chest. "We found it."

They attacked the adjacent floorboards, exposing more bundles. Each revealed stack sent electric currents through Tammy's spine. The money radiated untold stories of betrayal, murder, and justice delayed.

"Unbelievable." Wally's voice matched Tammy's thoughts.

Lockie bounded into the exposed hiding spot, sniffing at the bundles. Tammy smiled. Always the detective.

Joy bubbled inside Tammy like champagne, impossible to contain. She scooped Lockie from the hole and twirled.

"We did it!" she cried, as Lockie purred. After all the twists and turns, the little blue cottage had finally relinquished its ghosts. Max had forgotten nothing. In his own scrambled way, he had been telling them where the money was all along.

"Who would have thought?" Mrs. Temperance's voice floated through Tammy's euphoria. "All this time, right under our noses."

The team extracted stack after stack, creating a miniature skyline of cash in the center of the room. Tammy's fingers trembled as she added another bundle to the pile.

The cash spilled across the warped floorboards as they whooped and hollered, tossing bills into the air.

"We're rich!" Xander shouted.

As the frenzy faded, Lockie wiggled free from Tammy's arms and pounced back into the opening beneath the floorboards. He began pawing at something in the corner, letting out an insistent meow.

"What is it, boy?" Tammy reached in where Lockie was indicating. Her fingers brushed against something smooth and metallic. "There's something else here."

She pulled out an old cookie tin, its floral paint chipped but intact. "It's heavy."

"There's more," Olivia pointed, leaning over the opening. Tammy reached back in and retrieved another tin, then a third. One had tulips and the faded label *Holland's Best—Since 1912* curling around the edge. The other was navy blue with a lighthouse design and the words *Great Lakes Cookie Co.* in gold script.

"These are old," Mrs. Temperance observed, running her finger along the decorative edge of one tin. "Mother had ones just like these."

Tammy pried open the first lid, which gave way with a soft pop. Inside sat a stack of well-preserved handwritten letters.

"They're in perfect condition," she marveled, lifting one out. "The tins must have protected them all these years."

She unfolded the topmost sheet, the paper still crisp despite its age. The handwriting was faded but legible. As she read, understanding dawned.

"They're love letters...from Cathy... to Mary."

Mrs. Temperance's eyes widened. "You mean those two girls were..."

"More than friends," Olivia finished.

They spread the letters from all three tins across the floor, piecing together the puzzle that had led them to this moment. It became clear Mary and Cathy had robbed the bank to escape to the city, leaving their small-town lives behind.

"Wow," Xander breathed, scanning the words on the page. "I never would have guessed those two would go to such lengths for each other."

"Love makes people do crazy things," Mrs. Temperance said.

They continued to read in silence.

"They robbed the bank for a chance at a life," said Wally.

Tammy refolded a letter, picturing the two doomed women. "They took such a risk for love."

Mrs. Temperance sighed heavily. "If only they'd lived in different times. Then none of this would have happened."

The room fell silent, the old letters bringing the tragedy into focus. After all these years, Mary and Cathy's private love had come to light.

As they read through the heartfelt words, it became apparent Victor Walsh had played a role, albeit unintentionally.

"Victor must have bragged about his map," Xander speculated. "He probably thought it would impress Mary, and never considered it would be used for the heist."

"Talk about a twist," Tammy murmured, fixated on the delicate handwriting of one of the love letters.

"Seems like Victor's influence had unexpected consequences," Olivia noted, a thoughtful expression on her face.

"Indeed," Mrs. Temperance agreed. "This changes everything."

Tammy's brows knitted. "So, we had it all wrong before. We thought Max robbed the bank and Mary caught him, but it's clear now—Mary and Cathy did the heist."

"Max must have witnessed them with the money," said Olivia. "That's what his ramblings meant."

Wally nodded. "He confronted Mary, demanded to know where the money was hidden, and when she wouldn't tell him, he killed her in a rage. Victor interrupted, so Max never got the chance to search."

"Then Max targeted Cathy," Mrs. Temperance added. "And Cathy, in desperation, must've claimed the money was in the tunnels. When Max didn't find it there..."

"He killed Cathy," Tammy finished the sentence. "All of it is assumptions, but it fits."

"Max's letter might have been referring to their relationship," Olivia said.

"Did Max have nothing to do with it?" asked Xander.

"He murdered Mary; we've proven that," said Wally.

Mrs. Temperance released a heavy sigh.

"Mrs. T, what's wrong?" Xander asked, concern etched across his face.

The older woman glanced up from the letters with somber eyes. "It's so sad," she began, her voice cracking. "Mary and Cathy were victims of society. All of this happened because two women loved each other, and society said they couldn't be together. Those poor girls had to hide who they were. If society had been more accepting, they wouldn't have needed to steal money or run away."

Tammy placed a comforting hand on Mrs. Temperance's arm. "Love shouldn't bring pain, but it so often does." She recalled her own disastrous history with love.

Her gut wrenched. How cruel the world had been to Mary and Cathy. Forced to hide, driven to extremes, destroyed for wanting nothing more than love.

Lockie, observing the group from his spot on the windowsill, let out a soft mewl, as if sharing their collective grief. Tammy reached out to stroke his black-and-white fur, grateful for the comfort he provided.

Mrs. Temperance dabbed at her cheeks with a handkerchief. "We may never learn all the details, but they are now free."

While the precise mystery of how they got in and out of the bank was still unsolved, the discovery of the lost money and the details of Mary and Cathy's relationship added new depth to the story.

Tammy agreed. "If they'd been allowed to live their lives as they wanted, Victor would never have given Mary the map, and both Mary and Cathy might still be alive today. Even Nathan wouldn't have been arrested, as there wouldn't have been any bank heist money for him to search for."

"Such a waste," Olivia whispered, her heart aching for the love that had been torn apart by the unjust world in which they'd lived.

"Sometimes love can make people do desperate things," Mrs. Temperance said. "But it should never come at such a high cost."

Tammy raised a letter dated a few days after the robbery.

"Listen to this: 'Remember how we couldn't stop giggling as we rolled each wine barrel through the tunnel? And how one almost went rolling down the hill! We laughed until we were breathless.'"

"They got the money out in wine barrels?" asked Xander.

Chuckles rippled through the group at the image, dispersing the somber mood.

"There are a couple of barrels out back used as garden ornaments. Imagine if they were the barrels used in the heist," said Tammy.

"It must have been quite the adventure," said Mrs. T. "Two young lovers exploring underground passages, stumbling upon a fortune, and making off with the perfect heist."

"Let's make sure their story is told," Olivia said. "At least we can give them that."

"We should tell the sheriff," said Xander.

"Yes," Wally agreed. "They need to know."

Tammy clutched one of the letters. "Can we keep these letters to ourselves for now? Mary and Cathy's story is too personal to be shared with the world just yet."

"Tammy's right," Olivia said. "We can tell the authorities about the money and how it connects to the bank robbery, but keep the love letters out of it for now."

"Agreed," Mrs. Temperance said. "There will be time later to decide what to do with them, but for now, they deserve some privacy."

Chapter 20

The sound of speeding cars filled the air as two squad cars screeched to a halt in front of Tammy's blue cottage. Sheriff Stanton stepped out, and the team scrambled to hide the evidence.

Tammy grabbed the first decorative tin. "Stash the letters somewhere no one would ever look."

Olivia scanned the kitchen, landing on the pet supplies. "Here!" She snatched bags of Lockie's cat food and kitty litter.

They transferred the letters while Wally distracted the officers at the door, buying them time. The vintage biscuit tins now sat empty on a shelf—decorative items, nothing suspicious.

"Even if he opens them, they're empty now," Mrs. T whispered, tucking the last bundle of letters deep into a bag of kitty litter.

"Wallace, I'm going to have to give you a badge to keep you out of trouble," the sheriff said, shaking Wally's hand.

"Old habits die hard, Stan," Wally replied with a wry smile. "But I'm quite enjoying my life without a badge. Come let me show you what we've discovered."

Tammy held her breath behind pursed lips as the sheriff and Wally entered the attic stairwell opposite the kitchen. If only the sheriff knew what was happening behind him.

With the letters stashed away, Tammy and the others exited the kitchen to find deputies stationed everywhere.

"They've brought the cavalry," said Olivia.

Lockie sauntered around the newcomers, his tail held high as if inspecting intruders in his domain.

Tammy joined them in the attic. Sheriff Stanton's eyes were wide at the sight of the stacks of old banknotes.

"Good lord," he muttered in disbelief. "This is... this is the missing money from the bank heist, isn't it?"

"Seems so," Wally confirmed. "The trail led us here, and we found it under the floorboards."

Stanton took notes while a deputy snapped photos. He faced Tammy.

"This is a crime scene now," he said.

"I understand," she replied. Her home, the little blue cottage, was once again enveloped in yellow crime scene tape.

Deputies dusted for prints and bagged the money for evidence.

The decades-old mystery of the Willowcroft bank heist was finally solved. But, of course, it wasn't that simple. There were still loose ends.

"You'll be staying with me then, Tammy," Wally said.

"Thank you. Yes. I'll pack a bag for myself and Lockie."

Tammy gathered some essentials into a tote bag, including the cat food and kitty litter bags for Lockie. The little cat wound himself around her ankles, meowing.

"I know, I know, time to go," Tammy said, scooping him up. Lockie curled into the crook of her arm.

Wally waited by the front door, hands in his pockets. "All set?"

Tammy nodded, taking one last peek around the cozy cottage that had become a crime scene again. "Let's get out of the officers' way."

"Let's head to my place first," Olivia said. "We need to take in all this new information. And Mrs. T says she's got something to show us. We'll see you there soon."

Wally opened the passenger door of his sedan for Tammy. "Don't worry, you'll be back home before you know it."

Tammy settled into the front seat, clutching her bag in her lap. "It's just—this was supposed to be a fresh start. But the past is haunting me again. And it's not even my own past."

The secrets concealed within the walls of her home consumed her thoughts.

She thought about the love affair between Cathy and Mary, their daring bank heist, and the letter she found in the attic that started it all. It was as if the past had come alive, binding her to the story of the two women.

Olivia and Wally drove the team to Bookworm Haven.

Mrs. T was bouncing as Tammy and Wally walked through the bookcase door. "Come along now, I've got something to show you."

"Okay, Mrs. T, let's see what you've got," Wally said, rubbing his hands.

The team followed her into the back room. Xander organized the projector. Lockie leaped onto a nearby chair, his tail twitching with interest.

"Before I handed Victor's tunnel map over to the deputies," Mrs. Temperance began, "I took photos." She presented her smartphone with a grin.

"Mrs. T, you sly fox!" Olivia exclaimed, while the rest of the team applauded her ingenuity.

"Xander, dear, would you mind putting the photos on the projector?" Mrs. Temperance's phone dinged before she passed it to Xander.

"Sure thing, Mrs. T," Xander replied, transferring the images. The walls were soon illuminated with the detailed map of the town's underground tunnels.

A knock on the door halted their start, and a pizza delivery person greeted Olivia. Shocked, she took the boxes into the back room.

"Oh yeah," said Xander, "I ordered food while Tammy was packing."

Wally patted the young man on the back. "Excellent work son."

"Oh, and I called my parents. They are furious, so it's best I don't go home until they're calm."

Everyone stood eating as they scrutinized every inch of the map, larger than life on the screen.

Mrs. T's phone skimmed across the table.

She ignored it as she pointed at a section of the map. "The map shows a room off the bank vault. We've confirmed the middle safety deposit box room is smaller in real life, contrary to the original blueprint. This room must have an access point into the vault."

"Good job," Wally said, admiration in his voice.

"Thank you, dear," she replied, her cheeks flushing.

"If that's true," said Olivia. "They didn't need Cathy's bank access. It's a coincidence she worked there."

"They came in through the bank entrance from the tunnel," said Tammy, "and had full access to the bank's vault. And since it was 1954, there were no cameras, and the security guards would have been on the outside, out of sight."

"We did it!" Xander exclaimed, pumping his fist in the air. "We figured out how Mary and Cathy robbed the bank."

"And we were crediting Max all this time," said Wally.

"If it was a fake door like at the Swinging Spoon, they'd have been in and out within an hour or two, no planning required!" said Olivia.

"It was the perfect crime of *opportunity*," Wally said, shaking his head. "They stumbled upon a fortune and took it."

Olivia's eyes gleamed. "And rolled the money out in wine barrels."

Tammy let out a long, contented sigh. "What an incredible discovery. I can't believe those two pulled off such a daring heist."

She glanced at Lockie, who purred in her lap, pleased with the progress they were making.

"I can't believe how easily Mary and Cathy got away with it," said Xander.

"Well, they didn't, did they?" said Mrs. Temperance. "They both lost their lives."

"Mary and Cathy weren't just murder victims. They were bank robbers too," Wally said. "Not exactly innocent bystanders."

"True," Olivia agreed. "They were also victims of society, forced to hide who they were and what they wanted."

Xander spoke up. "Do you think we'll get a finder's fee for finding the money?"

Trust Xander to think ahead and be undeterred by societal norms.

"I mean, we uncovered a fortune in stolen cash."

Olivia swatted his arm playfully. "Don't be ridiculous. This wasn't about the money."

"We did this for the thrill of the hunt," Wally said. "For the chance to solve a mystery unsolved for seventy years."

"And for the opportunity to spend time with dear friends," Mrs. Temperance added.

"The whole thing's like something out of a novel," said Tammy.

"Or a movie," Olivia added. "Titled 'The Tunnels of Destiny' or something extra dramatic. Tammy could write it."

"Starring Lockie as the feline mastermind," Tammy joked, reaching to scratch the cat behind his ears.

Tammy smiled at the group of people gathered around her. They had embarked on an exciting adventure and formed unbreakable bonds along the way. That was worth far more than any finder's fee.

Wally raised his glass. "To friendship and mystery solving."

"To friendship and mystery solving!" they chorused, clinking glasses and reveling in the moment.

Chapter 21

Mrs. T's phone lit up.

"What is going on with your phone, Mrs. T?" Xander asked.

"You've created monsters. The Willow-Crafters group chat is constant. They won't stop texting."

Xander laughed. "You were the one who wanted me to teach you all."

"And I regret it."

"How are they doing? Are they getting things right?"

Mrs. T handed her phone to Xander. "See for yourself."

Xander read through the most recent chat messages:

Della Mae: Can I put in a request for lemon shortbread at our next meeting?

Marjorie: I'M ALMOST OUT OF YARN.

Beatrice: Marjorie, your caps lock is on.

Marjorie: WHAT? HOW DO I TURN IT OFF?

Betty: Try double-tapping the little arrow thingy on the keyboard!

Marjorie: Did that make it worse?

Della Mae: You're fine now. What's this about the radio station?

Marjorie: Greg Wescott had a complete meltdown on air, ranting about outsiders, then he cut to an ad mid-sentence. Very unprofessional. Though not unsurprising for that family.

Della Mae: He's been playing the same old records on repeat too.

Beatrice: He snapped at a caller on air.

Betty: He's secretly in love with someone and was having a dramatic moment!

Marjorie: It was NOT romantic, Betty. He sounded as jittery as a cat in a room full of rocking chairs.

Della Mae: He's nervous about the new festival broadcast they're planning. He was at the store yesterday buying a ridiculous amount of herbal tea. Boxes and boxes of it. Like he was stocking up for a year.

Marjorie: Why would a radio host need that much tea?

Beatrice: Marjorie, you once bought twenty pounds of flour on sale and said it was "for emergencies."

Betty: Ooooooh, he's planning a surprise tea party proposal!

Marjorie: Betty, I swear...

Della Mae: He was muttering to himself while paying. Katie had to repeat the total twice because he was so distracted.

Betty: What did he say?

Della Mae: I think it was something about "getting ahead of things." I struggled to hear. Behind me, Bea complained about how overpriced apples are this season.

Beatrice: They ARE! A dollar each for an apple? Ridiculous! Do you think Mrs. Applewood could get us a friend's discount from her brother at Parkland Orchards?

Xander handed back the phone. "They appear to be getting the hang of it."

The team's conversation had shifted while Xander was reading the chat, because the first thing he heard was Tammy saying, "But who killed Cathy?"

Chapter 22

The celebratory atmosphere sobered in an instant. They had solved the mystery of the heist, but Cathy's murder remained unsolved. If it was Cathy.

Tammy stared at the mess of papers and photographs spread across the table and began sifting through them, searching for the original attic letter.

"We always assumed the letter warned Mary about tying Max to the heist, but that theory no longer fits."

Her fingers brushed against the worn paper she was searching for. "Here it is. 'If anyone finds out, you'll get it. You better leave town or else.'"

"Which gave them even more incentive to steal the money and run away," Olivia concluded.

"Does that mean the threat came before the robbery?" Xander asked.

The room fell silent. Lockie curled up at Tammy's feet, a warm weight against her ankles as she tried to organize her thoughts.

"Max must have tried to leverage their relationship," she said. "Then the girls stole the money, and Max wanted it too."

She ran her fingers across the letter. "When they refused to give it to him..." She swallowed hard. "He killed Mary, hiding in the hollow behind my fireplace to escape capture."

"And Cathy?" Wally prompted.

Tammy hesitated. "If Max didn't know about the tunnels until Cathy showed him, maybe she thought leading him there would buy her time and save her life."

Mrs. Temperance shook her head. "But she never made it out. Eleanor said they never found the tunnels when they were children."

Wally's mouth tightened. "And Max didn't need to hide Cathy's body. The tunnels buried the evidence for him."

"Such a senseless waste," Mrs. Temperance murmured, her eyes glistening with unshed tears.

"Nathan's notebook proves Max knew about the money," said Tammy, "but not how he learned it. After all these years, with everyone involved being dead, we're unlikely to know every detail."

"Sometimes, uncovering the stories of those who can no longer speak for themselves is more important than solving the crime," Mrs. Temperance said.

Tammy sighed. "More assumptions we have to live with, I guess."

She ticked off the facts on her fingers. "We know Mary and Cathy did the heist because they say so in their letters. We know Max killed Mary from DNA evidence on the knife."

"We assume Max discovered their relationship," added Olivia, "and tried to blackmail them into leaving. When they didn't give him the money, he killed them both."

Wally frowned. "And still never found the money."

"All those ramblings in Nathan's notebook were Max chasing ghosts," Xander said. "He never figured it out."

Tammy rubbed her temples. "Even Max was guessing."

Another question stirred. "If Mary and Cathy had the map, how did Victor's descendants get it?"

"Victor loves hanging around our suspects list," said Mrs. Temperance.

"Maybe he was at the cottage the night Mary died to get the map back," Tammy suggested. "The sheriff wouldn't have taken any notice of a map in his pocket. He couldn't have understood its relevance."

"Or he hid it," Olivia said, "as one final gift to Mary."

"You're as bad as Betty with your romantic notions," said Mrs. T.

"Let's not forget," Tammy chimed in, "that we found Cathy's skeleton in the tunnels. It makes sense she lured Max down there."

"Or tried to trap him," Mrs. Temperance suggested. "But it cost her life."

Lockie let out a plaintive meow. Tammy gathered him into her arms, her heart breaking. So much loss and tragedy. But at least now, she understood.

"It's a tragic story," Mrs. T said. "But we've given Mary and Cathy closure. Regardless of how it all played out, we can't change the past."

"We will not learn anything more tonight," Wally said, stifling a yawn.

"It is getting late," Tammy said, becoming aware of her own exhaustion. "We should get some sleep."

"I don't want to go home. My parents are furious," said Xander.

"Don't tell me they don't know where you are," said Wally.

"I thought you were all in danger and that I was the only one who knew where you might be. I had to sneak out."

"You're all good, Xander. The station called about coming in for a sound check tomorrow morning, and I rang your parents to get permission. They know where you are. I think they are so excited about you getting accepted into the show that they've forgotten about you sneaking out."

"I got in?"

"The comedy show saved you from getting into trouble," said Olivia.

"I think I'd rather be in trouble with my parents."

"Don't be silly," said Mrs. T. "You'll be fine. Can I come to the sound check? I'd love to go behind the scenes of the studio."

"Sure," said Xander. "I'm going to need all the support I can get."

Mrs. T gave a single clap. "Excellent."

"Tammy and I can mind the store if you need," offered Wally.

"That would be great. We shouldn't be long, but if you're here, I can open as usual and we can duck out when it's time."

"Time for me to die," Xander groaned.

"It's a sound check," Tammy reassured him. "What could go wrong?"

Tammy gathered Lockie into her arms. "All I know is I need to rest. Thank you for letting me stay at yours, Wally. Let's call it a night."

He smiled, squeezing her shoulder. "Of course."

Wally offered to drive everyone home. As they stepped out of the bookstore, the cool night air greeted Tammy with a soft breeze, bringing goosebumps to her arms. The soft chirping of crickets prompted her to gaze at the moon casting a silvery glow over Willowcroft's quiet streets. Behind her, Olivia's key clicked the bookstore's lock.

As Mrs. Temperance opened the car door, a bright ping sounded from the older woman's handbag. Mrs. T pulled out her phone and frowned at the screen, then let out a small "oh my" under her breath. Several more pings followed in rapid succession.

"Everything all right?" Tammy asked.

Mrs. Temperance gave a quick, amused shake of her head. "It seems the Willow-Crafters have heard about our discovery." She slipped the phone into her bag.

After dropping Mrs. T across the square and Xander at his parents' house, Wally and Tammy made their way to his place. It made sense for Tammy to stay there—she needed somewhere to sleep, and someone needed to monitor him with that head injury.

Wally winced as he touched his bandage.

"If Andrew Walsh is telling the truth, we still don't know who attacked you," Tammy said, settling onto his comfortable couch.

"I've been thinking the same thing." Wally lowered himself into his recliner. "He did appear as if he was telling the truth about not being involved."

"Who else is left?"

"Multiple descendants have hung up on us. It could have been any of them."

Chapter 23

Notty but Nice Group Chat

[2:15 PM]

Betty: DID EVERYONE HEAR THE NEWS???? MONEY FOUND IN THE BLUE COTTAGE!!

Marjorie: Betty, why are you shouting?

Betty: SORRY! Excitement got the better of me! Oops, there I go again!

Della Mae: How much money was it? Katie wouldn't tell me at Mrs. Hubbard's earlier. She said she was sworn to secrecy, but kept smiling.

Marjorie: Katie says everyone in Willowcroft is talking about it. She can't keep the shelves stocked! People are buying things just to hang around and gossip. She told me it was close to three hundred thousand dollars. Not exactly a king's ransom these days, but nothing to sneeze at either. That girl needs to learn to keep her mouth shut.

Beatrice: To think how many tenants have lived in the little blue cottage over seventy years, and not one of them found the money! My nephew Brian lived there in '86 and never noticed a thing!

Della Mae: I heard from Katie, who heard from her delivery boy, that Sheriff Stanton is looking mighty nervous about all this. Something about "chain of custody" and "legal precedent."

Betty: Hazel! Does Tammy get to keep it? That would be just like a movie!

Della Mae: Hazel's probably with Tammy and the others figuring all this out.

Betty: Ooooh, that's right! She has the inside scoop!

Beatrice: What else are they saying at the Cupboard?

Marjorie: Old man Caldwell swore up and down that his uncle confessed on his deathbed that he knew who did it.

Della Mae: People are saying the money was stacked nice and neat under the floorboards in the attic. Is that true, Hazel?

[3:00 PM]

Della Mae: Hazel has answered none of our messages.

Beatrice: I heard from my niece a bank manager from Detroit is coming to examine the bills. Something about serial numbers.

Betty: It's like we're living in an Agatha Christie novel! So thrilling!

Marjorie: Betty, settle down. Though I will say, my father-in-law always said there was something fishy about old Mayor Whitfield. He bought a big house in Florida.

Della Mae: Marjorie! You can't just accuse a former mayor!

Beatrice: How do I delete a message someone else sent? This is slander.

Marjorie: It's not slander if it's true. Henry Hubbard kept meticulous records of town finances, but the numbers never added up!

Betty: Do you think there's a curse on the money? That's why Mary Collins died?

Della Mae: I dropped my knitting. A curse? Really, Betty?

Marjorie: The only curse is the one I'm holding back right now.

Beatrice: Maxine texted. She's digging out the old newspaper articles about the heist. She says there's a line out the door, so she's keeping the library open late tonight.

Betty: We should go! Emergency Willow-Crafters field trip!

Della Mae: Has Hazel contacted anyone?

Betty: What if the money was hidden by aliens?

Marjorie: I'm turning my phone off.

Marjorie has left the chat.

Betty: Where did Marjorie go?

Della Mae: Hazel must still be with Tammy and the others.

Betty: This is the most exciting thing to happen since the possum got stuck in the church organ!

[4:30 PM]

Marjorie has rejoined the chat.

Marjorie: That was a raccoon, Betty. And I was talking to Katie, who says Sheriff Stanton has the cash locked in the evidence room. He's even sleeping at the station to guard it.

Betty: Marjorie! You came back!

Marjorie: I had to correct that possum nonsense. And share what Katie told me.

Betty: Hazel. Are you there, Hazel???

Betty: Do you think there are more treasures in old houses around town? We should check our attics!

Marjorie: I checked mine. Nothing but Christmas decorations and Gerald's bowling trophies.

Betty: We should start a town holiday—Willowcroft Treasure Day!

Marjorie: Betty, for heaven's sake. I'm turning my phone off again.

Betty: Wait! I found a new button! What does this do?

Betty has shared her location.

Della Mae: Betty, you just showed us all where you are.

Betty: I'm at home knitting! Now you all know!

Marjorie: I'm definitely turning my phone off now.

[5:00 PM]

Betty: I'm going to Mrs. Hubbard's for more gossip! Who's coming with me?

Della Mae: I'll meet you there in ten minutes.

Marjorie: ...I'll be there in five. Someone needs to keep you two from spreading wild tales.

[8:00 PM]

Betty: HAZEL?

Marjorie: At her age, she might have put her phone in the fridge again.

Betty: HAZEL IF YOU CAN READ THIS TEXT BACK

Della Mae: Betty, it's not a hostage situation.

Marjorie: No, but it is Hazel. She is probably processing everyone's nonsense.

Hazel smiled as she scrolled through the messages—it was all so... them.

She sipped her tea and chuckled, warmth blooming in her chest. The town was buzzing, and the Willow-Crafters were positively vibrating.

She tapped out a reply with careful fingers.

[10:00 PM]

Hazel: Apologies for the silence. I've just settled in with my tea and caught up on all your theories. I'll tell you everything at the next Willow-Crafters meeting.

Chapter 24

The next morning, Tammy's back screamed as she climbed out of Wally's grandchildren's bunk bed. She'd tossed and turned all night, the narrow mattress a poor substitute for her own bed. It wasn't her first night seeking refuge in the room, but it was the first time alone with Wally in his bedroom along the hall.

Muffled groans seeped through the thin walls throughout the night. Twice she'd swung her legs over the side of the bed, ready to check on him, but stopped. Men like Wally hated being seen as vulnerable. This morning, she'd caught him slipping a pill bottle into his pocket when he thought she wasn't looking, his hands trembling as he tried to hide it.

They arrived at the bookstore just as Olivia flipped the sign to "Open."

Mrs. Temperance swept in behind them, wrapped in a vibrant blue shawl matching the sky outside. She sidled next to Tammy while Wally shuffled toward the back room.

"How's he doing?" she whispered, setting her handbag on the counter.

"Better, but still sore." Tammy bit back mentioning the pill bottle bulging in Wally's jacket pocket. "He needs rest, but you know Wally."

"He's too stubborn for his own good," Mrs. Temperance clucked.

While Mrs. T hovered behind Wally as they disappeared into the back room, Tammy caught Olivia's attention. "How did last night's project go after we left?"

Olivia gave a triumphant smile. "All taken care of," she whispered. "Both digital and hard copies are tucked away. I stayed awake half the night reading the letters, though." She removed her glasses to clean them, revealing dark circles.

"Thank you for doing that." Tammy squeezed her friend's arm. "I feel better knowing there are copies. We won't be able to keep them to ourselves forever, but with backups, we'll always have access."

"Their story was even more beautiful than I imagined. Cathy had quite a way with words. But do you know what struck me reading them in order?"

Tammy shook her head.

"It was so one-sided. I wish we had Mary's letters to Cathy."

Tammy headed into the back room, leaving Olivia alone in the store. She'd barely settled when the bookcase door creaked open, pulling her attention. Olivia stepped through, with Peter Walsh trailing behind. His gray hair lay combed against his scalp. His eyes landed on the murder board, and his fingers twitched at his sides.

Olivia closed the door behind them.

Tammy set down her pen. "What brings you here today, Mr. Walsh?"

"Please call me Peter." He stepped into the room, shoulders sagging. "I came to apologize. For Andrew. My son."

"Apologize for what *exactly?*" Wally's voice hardened.

Peter flinched. "What he did to you all in the tunnel. Locking you in there was dangerous and inexcusable." He ran a hand through his hair. "Andrew confessed everything when I confronted him at the sheriff's about his sneaking off. I'm mortified. That's not how we raised him."

Wally crossed his arms. "And the threatening letters?"

"He said nothing about any letters," Peter said, wincing. "I've never been so disappointed in him."

"Why would he do such a thing?" Mrs. Temperance asked.

"The money." Peter's voice dropped. "Ever since he discovered some of my father's old papers mentioning the bank heist..."

"So you knew about your father's connection?" Tammy stepped closer.

"I'd heard rumors." Peter's gaze fell to the floor. "Victor wasn't forthcoming about his past, but things slipped out when I was a child. Then there were those years he was away—1955 to 1957."

"The years Tammy asked about during our visit," Mrs. Temperance said.

"Victor was dating Mary Collins when she died in '54." His hands trembled. "Her murder broke something in him. The town believed he'd done it, and despite swearing his innocence, he always blamed himself."

"Why would he blame himself if he didn't kill her?" Tammy interrupted.

Peter stiffened. "I wish I knew. After Mary's death, he spent those missing years in a mental institution. He met my mother, Helen, working as a nurse there. They married after his release."

A pang shot through Tammy's chest. The past was harsh and unforgiving when it came to mental health struggles. People disappeared into institutions back then, sometimes never to return. Yet somehow Victor had found love amid the darkness.

"Their relationship caused quite the scandal," Peter continued, shaking his head. "A nurse marrying her former patient wasn't the norm. But they were happy."

"And the map?" Wally cut in. "The one Andrew gave us in the tunnel."

"I'd intended to share it with you the day you visited." Peter straightened. "But Andrew pulled me aside. He insisted on keeping the map."

"The whispering we heard," Tammy said.

"Yet Andrew gave us the map anyway," Mrs. Temperance pointed out. "Why?"

Peter's laughter was short and bitter. "Not out of kindness. He thought if he gave you the map, you'd do the hard work of finding the money, and then he would take it from you."

"That's why he locked us in," Tammy said. "He wanted us to do the dangerous part."

"I'm sorry," Peter said.

"These actions put people in danger," Wally said.

"He's being punished, believe me." Peter's voice dropped. "I've insisted he write personal apologies to each of you. He's just a boy who got caught up in a treasure hunt."

"What about the fake newspaper article? The attack in Stonefield?" Wally pressed, his face tightening.

"He swears he had nothing to do with that." Peter's eyes met Wally's. "I'd sent him to Stonefield for errands, but he was home by four p.m."

Wally and Tammy exchanged glances.

"Whatever you find—if there is money—it doesn't belong to my family," Peter said. "It was stolen. I have no claim to it."

"Does Andrew feel the same?" Mrs. Temperance raised an eyebrow.

"He will, once I'm through with him." Peter shifted his attention around the back room. "I'll let you get back to your work."

With a nod, he stepped into the store. The bookcase door creaked shut, and moments later, the distant chime of the main door signaled his departure.

"This mystery seems determined to keep us on our toes," Mrs. Temperance said.

"We still have work to do," Wally said, dabbing at his bandage.

Olivia pinned a note on the board: IF NOT ANDREW OR PETER... THEN WHO?

Wally dabbed at his bandage, wincing.

"And why are Victor, Clark, and Samuel in Nathan's notebook at all?" Tammy asked. "Did Max mention them in his rambles?"

"Seems odd, doesn't it?" Wally shifted in his chair. "We haven't tied them back to Max."

"Victor dating Mary explains his name," Tammy said, "but the others?"

Olivia tapped the page. "I found a book about the Michaels family during Prohibition. It suggests all three families—Walsh, Michaels, and Grey—were involved."

"They all knew about the tunnels!" Xander said.

"If Cathy told Max the money was in the tunnels, after he killed her, he needed someone who knew them to help find it," Mrs. Temperance concluded.

"Prohibition would have been recent history in 1954," Tammy added. "People would have known the families involved."

"Eleanor confirmed she and Max never found the tunnels," Mrs. T said. "Nathan drove himself mad believing the money was at the cottage. He didn't know the tunnels existed—he was following Max's scrambled memories, not real clues. He couldn't have added those family names from his own research because he didn't know why Max mentioned them."

"Max only discovered the tunnels when Cathy showed him," Olivia said. "With Cathy dead, he needed information those families had."

"Let's examine the facts." Wally grabbed a marker. "Max killed Mary. Mary and Cathy pulled off the bank heist using Prohibition tunnels. We've found the money."

"The money was at the blue cottage the whole time," Tammy added. "We didn't need the tunnels to find it."

"And Cathy's letters explained everything," Olivia said. "The three families were a wild goose chase. Max must have latched onto them later, desperate for a clue."

"His rambles weren't clues," Wally said. "They were memories, fragmented and repeated, like a story he kept trying to finish but couldn't."

"A giant cut-and-paste puzzle stuffed with fill-in-the-blank holes," Xander said.

"When you put it that way, it sounds impossible to know what Max did or what he knew," Olivia groaned.

"So, we are saying the families were important to Max because he never found the money," Xander said. "But they are irrelevant to us."

"They led us to the descendants and thus the tunnel map," Olivia said.

Wally stood, marker in hand. "I think we can officially cross the Walsh, Grey, and Michaels families off our suspect list." He drew bold lines through their names on the board. "They were side characters in this story, not perpetrators."

"That eliminates all the descendants too," Mrs. T said.

"So who attacked Wally?" Xander asked.

Chapter 25

Xander would rather continue working on the mystery, but Olivia had theatrically announced it was time for his sound check and pushed him out the door. Wally and Tammy were watching the store.

The fluorescent lights of the Waves of Willowcroft radio station hummed overhead. Xander trudged behind Olivia and Mrs. T, his sneakers squeaking against the linoleum floor. His laptop bag bounced against his hip with each step—his emotional support computer, essentially.

"This is going to be great," Olivia chirped, walking backward to face him. "Your jokes are funny."

"To you maybe," Xander muttered. "Normal people don't laugh at teenage jokes." He shook his head. A comedy segment. Somehow, Olivia had volunteered him for this without asking—a classic case of friendship extortion if there ever was one. His palms were sweating more than a snowman in July at the thought of his voice traveling across Willowcroft, reaching the ears of classmates who already thought he was one firmware update short of normal.

Greg Wescott sat behind his desk. His movements reminded Xander of those corrupted animation files he'd tried to recover last month—jerky, unpredictable, all wrong. Greg's eyes darted everywhere except at their small group when they entered, as if they were IRS agents instead of a teenager and two women.

Where was the smooth, mellow-voiced guy who narrated Willowcroft's morning commute? This Greg buzzed with nervous energy, as if he'd downed five energy drinks but still laser-focused.

"Hey, um, thanks for having me," Xander said, adjusting his glasses as they attempted their hourly escape down the bridge of his nose.

Greg's head snapped toward them as if he'd been shocked. "Right. Yes. Sound check for the teen segment." His fingers drummed an erratic pattern against the desktop as he shuffled papers around. "We'll get you set up in a minute."

Mrs. T settled into a visitor chair, pulling out her ever-present knitting project. "No rush, Gregory. We're early anyway."

Greg's desk looked like the aftermath of an office supply tornado—papers scattered as if they'd had a fight with each other, used coffee mugs forming their own little civilization, and technical equipment arranged in what could only be described as "panic décor." A tower of tea boxes teetered on the corner of his desk, resembling a failed Jenga tournament.

Xander lifted a box to show Mrs. T. "The ones Mrs. Beasley mentioned in the group text."

Mrs. T acknowledged the tea but said nothing, her needles clicking.

As Xander returned the box, something underneath the tea captured his attention.

The paper. His brain processed the visual input like a high-resolution scanner: cream-colored, rough texture. The kind he'd seen folded into threatening notes.

"Sound check time," the studio tech called out from the control room door. "We need levels before the commercial break ends."

Greg jumped. "Yes. Coming." He herded Xander toward the recording booth with bulldozer subtlety. "Let's go, kid."

He couldn't grab the evidence now. Not without alerting him.

Think, Xander. Think.

Olivia shot him a look—like she knew something was wrong—but he had no choice.

The soundproofed door sealed behind them with a soft pneumatic hiss.

Trapped.

Glass and foam walls between him and help.

The booth reeked of coffee and something sharper—fear sweat? His dad would recognize it.

Was Olivia sure there wasn't a tunnel entrance behind the back wall? It might be useful right about now.

"Put these on," Greg said, thrusting a pair of headphones at him. "Stand about six inches from the mic."

Xander's hands shook as he fiddled with the professional head-phones—heavier than his gaming set and clearly built for radio people, not teenagers who'd been roped into comedy against their will.

Through the glass, Olivia gave him an enthusiastic thumbs-up that screamed, "I got you into this mess, and I'm not even sorry!" Mrs. T paused her knitting, her keen eyes tracking Greg's movements.

Greg's knee bounced up and down, creating a visible rhythm of anxiety. His fingers tapped the console, out of sync with his leg. Sweat beaded on his upper lip.

Xander had seen nervous people before—heck, he *was* one—but Greg was something else.

Was Greg involved?

"Testing, testing. Please read line one when you're ready, Xander," the producer's voice crackled through the headset with the cheerfulness of someone who wasn't trapped in a glass box with a potential criminal.

Xander couldn't focus on the script card. His brain processed the evidence like debugging code.

The threatening letters.

Wally's attack—blunt force trauma.

The fake newspaper article luring Wally to Stonefield Library.

None admitted to by Andrew Walsh.

Greg's strange behavior over the radio earlier in the week, at Mrs. Hubbard's Cupboard, and now.

The identical stationery.

"Uh... guys? Everything okay in there?" The producer's voice cut through the headphones.

The commercial break countdown flashed above the console.

10...

9...

8...

Greg zeroed in on each number, his eyes widening with each second.

"You've missed your slot, Xander. Jump out before we go live."

3...

2...

The chime played.

Live mic.

"You're behind the letters, the fake newspaper article, and Wally's attack?" Xander's words hit the airwaves like a system crash.

Greg's face went blue-screen-of-death blank. His hand slapped at the console buttons like someone force-quitting a program. "What? Cut the feed!" His voice spiked higher, broadcasting panic to every radio in Willowcroft. "I never attacked anyone at the library!"

Xander recognized the error message in Greg's words immediately. Classic information leak. "Didn't mention where the attack happened, Greg."

Every listener in town heard that.

Greg's mouth opened and closed like a computer trying to reboot after a crash. His focus jittered between the door, the mic, and Xander.

"You sent those threatening letters to scare us off, created a fake newspaper article about a bank heist in Stonefield to lure Wally to the library, and then attacked him from behind." Xander's voice steadied as he laid out the logic, like debugging broken code step by step. "All because we were getting close to the truth."

Greg slammed his chair backward. It crashed into the wall with a sound like dropped hardware. "You little—" His movements glitched as he lunged for the booth door.

But Mrs. T moved with the speed of someone auditioning for "Senior Citizen Ninjas," blocking his path, her knitting needles raised like makeshift weapons, points gleaming under the studio lights.

"I wouldn't, Gregory," she warned.

Greg stumbled back, bumping into Xander. His focus snapped to the control room—his last escape route. He scrambled toward it, knocking equipment to the floor like a failed hardware cascade.

"System failure," Xander thought, watching Greg's desperate escape attempt. Complete meltdown.

The producer snapped into action, lunging for the controls. Before he cut the feed, a new voice filled the studio.

"Greg Wescott, hands where I can see them."

Sheriff Stanton and Deputy Brown stood in the doorway, hands hovering near holstered weapons. The sheriff's expression remained as unreadable as encrypted data, but a flicker of triumph lit Deputy Brown's face.

"We heard everything," Stanton said.

Greg's shoulders collapsed. Air escaped him in one defeated exhale.

The producer killed the live feed by cutting to a song. The unmistakable bassline of "Under Pressure" kicked in. *Oh, real subtle.*

"What threatening letters? What newspaper article?" Stanton demanded, glancing between Xander, Olivia, and Mrs. T.

"Five threatening notes," Xander explained, grabbing the notepad from Greg's desk. "Each of us got one. The notepad gave it away. The same paper. Greg sent warnings to back off from investigating the bank heist."

"And made a fake article about a heist at Stonefield's bank," Olivia added. "He planted it at my bookstore where we'd see it."

"I sent it on purpose!" Greg blurted. "I needed neutral ground, somewhere quiet. Couldn't believe my luck with Wally arriving at the library on his own not long before closing."

Stanton's jaw tightened. "And why are these threats and this setup only reaching me now?"

Mrs. T lowered her knitting needles but maintained her position. "Oh, Greg... did you really think you'd scare us off?"

"You don't understand!" His voice was frantic now. "You people dig through the past like it's your playground. But it's my family you're ripping open. If you'd stopped, none of this would've happened!"

Deputy Brown moved forward with handcuffs while Sheriff Stanton read Greg his rights.

"You don't know what it's like," Greg snapped, "growing up with people whispering your family was crooked." His voice splintered. "The rumors. The suspicion. The town always blamed my grandfather and my entire family for anything and everything that happened, even when there was no proof."

Greg shook his head. "I thought... I thought if I found the money first... it'd be mine. No one would tie it back to my grandfather, and I'd leave this town forever."

"Oh, dear," said a calm Mrs. T. "Your grandfather was never involved."

Greg stumbled back like she'd slapped him.

"What?"

Olivia didn't flinch. "We've proved it. He was innocent, Greg. You attacked Wally to protect a secret that didn't exist."

Greg's face twisted. Anger. Confusion. Regret.

The sheriff's attention snapped between them. "Proved it? You have proof Cross robbed the bank?"

Xander's stomach dropped. System error. Olivia's eyes widened—a micro-expression most would miss.

"It wasn't Max Cross," Mrs. T said. "The actual culprits were quite unexpected."

Stanton's jaw tensed, a muscle jumping beneath the stubble. "When were you planning to share this revelation with law enforcement?"

"Tomorrow," Xander improvised, his voice cracking. "We were, um, collating all the evidence."

Stanton's eyebrows lifted so high they nearly disappeared under his hairline. "Evidence. You have physical evidence of a seventy-year-old cold case, and you're just mentioning it now?"

"It's... complicated," Olivia offered.

Deputy Brown secured Greg's handcuffs. "More complicated than a live radio confession?"

"Yes," Mrs. T said with such conviction that even Xander almost believed there was a good reason they'd withheld the information.

Stanton massaged his temples. It reminded Xander of his mother when he'd deleted her entire contacts list, trying to "optimize" her phone.

"All of you," Stanton said, each syllable measured, "will meet me at the station in one hour with whatever evidence you've gathered. And I mean all of it—threatening letters, fake articles, everything. Five victims of written threats in my jurisdiction without a single report. This isn't a game. Clear?"

Agreement crackled through the group without a word.

"Deputy, process Mr. Wescott. I'll handle our... amateur investigators." The word 'amateur' sounded like malware in his mouth.

The sheriff paused at the doorway to deliver one last glare that downloaded a simple message: one hour or else.

Xander's legs destabilized. The adrenaline crash hit like a power outage, and he gripped the console edge.

His eyes locked with Olivia's. She nodded once—the universal acknowledgment for "you solved a crime on live radio."

But her slight head tilt afterward added new data: "And now we're in big trouble."

An hour later, Olivia clutched the cat food bag against her chest as if it contained first editions instead of love letters. Her fingertips pressed against the plastic, tracing the faint outline of paper treasures within—Mary and Cathy's private world, preserved between folds of decades-old stationery.

"I still don't think we should do this," she said to Tammy as they approached the Sheriff's Department.

The afternoon sun baked the sidewalk, heating her anxiety to a rolling boil. "These women entrusted their words to secrecy. We're serving them up on a platter."

Xander's lanky frame hunched as though carrying a physical weight. "They've been quiet for seventy years. It's time they had a voice."

Olivia bristled. Easy for him to say. He hadn't spent hours poring over each intimate word, each desperate plan for escape. "Their love was never meant for public consumption."

"When you put it like that, it sounds worse than it is," Tammy said, nudging Olivia.

Mrs. T clutched her ever-present knitting bag closer. "History deserves truth, dear. Even when it's uncomfortable."

Wally pushed open the station door, the bell jangling with what sounded to Olivia like judgment. "We have the copies. Their story won't disappear."

Lockie trotted in ahead of them, tail high like a fuzzy periscope, unbothered by the tension. The cat made himself at home, rubbing against Deputy Brown's pant leg. He could never understand what Olivia was experiencing.

Sheriff Stanton stood near the dispatch desk, his face hardening when he spotted the team. Then a hint of a smile at their unusual cargo.

"That was... unexpected. But effective," he said. "I'm glad we found our culprit, thanks to your quick thinking on air." His expression shifted to confusion as he gestured to their bags. "But why are you all standing here with pet supplies instead of the evidence you mentioned?"

"This is the evidence," Tammy said, lifting the kitty litter bag slightly.

Stanton stared at her. "You hid evidence in cat food bags?"

"We needed a quick hiding place at Tammy's when the deputies arrived," Wally explained. "These were convenient."

"They're letters," Olivia added. "Love letters between Mary and Cathy that reveal they were the ones who committed the bank heist."

Stanton's eyes widened. "Love letters? Between the two women?"

Olivia's grip tightened on the bag. "Yes. And they're private. These women—" She stopped, catching herself. "It's not just about the heist."

Her fingers refused to release their hold. These weren't evidence; they were Mary and Cathy's hearts poured onto paper, confessions of love in an era that would have destroyed them.

"I made copies," she said. "Digital scans. Here's your proof." Reluctantly, she extended the bag.

"You mean evidence smuggled out of a crime scene?" Stanton stared at the cat food bag as he took it.

Lockie meowed, jumping onto the counter and sitting like a sphinx, seemingly pleased with his role as unwitting accomplice.

Mrs. T stepped forward, her posture straight despite her years. "Sheriff, these women lived in fear. They died in fear. The least we can do is treat their memories with dignity."

Stanton's cheek muscles twitched. "The originals, Ms. Huddlestone."

"You don't understand what's in these letters." Her voice sharpened like a just-honed knife. "They deserve dignity. Their relationship was—"

"Their relationship is no longer my primary concern," Stanton cut through her protest. "Civilians withholding crucial evidence is."

Wally stepped forward. "Stanton, if I—"

"Not now, Wally." Stanton pinched the bridge of his nose. "I expected better from all of you."

The disappointment in his voice stung worse than anger would have. Olivia's cheeks burned.

Deputy Brown took the cat litter bag from Tammy. "Is this—?"

"Evidence," Stanton finished.

Tammy sighed. "We found the letters with the money. They detail how Mary Collins and Cathy Robinson executed the bank heist in 1954. They were in love, Sheriff. They took the money to escape town."

The room fell silent. Even Lockie stopped washing his paw mid-lick.

"You're telling me two women robbed the bank, not Max Cross?" Stanton's incredulity seasoned every word. "And then what? Mary was killed for it?"

"We think Max discovered their relationship," Mrs. T said. "Blackmailed Mary over it. And Cathy—"

"Is likely our skeleton in the tunnels," Olivia finished, the words bitter as burnt coffee on her tongue.

Olivia relinquished her grip on the bag, sliding it across the counter. "Read them yourself. It's all there. It wasn't planned. They explored the tunnels and found an entrance into the bank. A crime of opportunity to escape Willowcroft."

"And you hid this evidence in cat supplies?" Brown asked, poking at the bag as if it might bite.

"The perfect hiding place," Wally said. "Who looks through cat litter?"

Lockie let out an indignant meow, as if offended by the suggestion.

Stanton opened the cat food, extracting a plastic bag. His fingers moved with surprising gentleness as he unfolded the first letter.

Olivia couldn't watch. She turned to the window, tracking a cardinal hopping along the sill. She'd spent all night with those letters, savoring each word, each declaration of a love that dared not speak its name. How Mary wrote about Cathy's eyes "reflecting moonlight like twin lakes." How Cathy promised to "build a life where we need never hide again"—a forbidden recipe ending in tragedy.

"Well, I'll be," Stanton said after several minutes.

"Now you understand," Olivia said.

He nodded. "I understand why you wanted to protect them. I also understand that you obstructed justice."

"Their love was criminalized enough in their time," Olivia said. "They don't need history remembering them only as thieves."

Stanton looked up from the letters, something unreadable in his expression. "They won't be remembered that way."

"No?"

"No." He gathered the letters. "They'll be remembered as the women who pulled off the most notorious heist in Michigan's history. That's a hell of a love story."

Lockie meowed loudly, as if in agreement, rubbing against the evidence bags with proprietary affection.

"I need official statements from all of you," Stanton continued. "And these letters are going into evidence."

Olivia swallowed the lump in her throat. "The copies—"

"I don't care about them," Stanton said. "But these originals belong to this investigation."

A hand found Olivia's shoulder—Tammy's. A silent squeeze of understanding.

Mrs. T smiled, her face creasing with warmth. "Some stories need the right time to be told."

Xander leaned against the wall, appearing both relieved and troubled. "What happens now?"

"Now," Stanton said, placing the letters in evidence bags, "we rewrite history. Max Cross downgrades to murderer only. And we put names to crimes seventy years cold with undisputed proof."

As Stanton disappeared into the evidence room, letters in hand, Olivia's chest tightened. She exhaled slowly, her shoulders dropping an inch. The letters, Cathy's neat block letters, would now live in plastic bags and manila folders.

Tagged.

Numbered.

Archived between police reports and crime scene photos. Their private whispers of "my darling" and "when we're free" would be pawed through by strangers who'd never understand what it meant to love in shadows.

Yet somewhere beneath her ribs, a knot loosened. Their story would breathe in daylight after seventy years of darkness as a testament to what people would risk for love.

Lockie jumped from the counter, stretching languidly before padding over to wind between Olivia's ankles. His purr vibrated against her skin, a slight comfort in the face of surrendering something precious.

"You did right," Mrs. T whispered, her aged hand patting Olivia's arm. "Sometimes the truth is the most powerful love letter of all."

Chapter 26

The following morning, Hazel's bones ached from all the recent excitement. The case might be closed, but loose ends still tugged at her conscience. Eleanor Bennett deserved to hear the full truth, even the painful parts. With this thought driving her forward, Hazel reached for her crimson shawl and set out for Serenity Gardens.

Hazel adjusted her crimson shawl—the one with golden tassels that always reminded her of fall leaves—before entering Serenity Gardens. Antiseptic mingled with the aroma of baking bread from the dining hall.

She'd volunteered here long enough to know the staff by name, the creak in the third-floor hallway, and which residents liked a second cup of tea. But she never quite got used to the underlying melancholy of a place where people came to live out their final years.

"Mrs. T!" Nurse Emma waved from the nurses' station, her scrubs adorned with cartoon octopuses wearing graduation caps. "Twice in one week? Eleanor must be extra lucky."

"Following up on our little mystery," Hazel said. "Any changes with Eleanor?"

Emma's smile dimmed. "Good days and bad days. Today seems decent—clearer than yesterday, at least. She's been asking for you."

"That's something, then."

"Oh! Almost forgot." Emma rummaged through a drawer and produced a small envelope. "She wanted to give you this. Said it was important you see it before you talk."

Hazel accepted the envelope. "Thank you, dear. Those are festive scrubs."

"Education week," Emma beamed, straightening her top. "The residents love them. Mr. Hill said the octopuses remind him of his Navy days."

Hazel slipped the envelope into her handbag and followed the hall toward Eleanor's room. She'd visited countless times, but today, every footfall carried the weight of the unearthed truths.

She knocked on the half-open door. "Eleanor? It's Hazel."

The room was warmer than the hallway, the afternoon sun streaming through the lace curtains. Eleanor sat by the window, a blanket draped across her knees despite the warmth. Someone had arranged her wispy white hair in an elegant style, probably Emma.

"Hazel." Eleanor's face brightened as she smiled. "You came back."

"I promised I would." Hazel crossed the room and settled into the visitor's chair. "You've been busy—your hair's lovely."

Eleanor's hand fluttered to her hair. "Emma fancies herself a stylist. I humor her." Her expression sharpened. "Did you read it?"

"Read what, dear?"

"The letter. I asked Emma to give it to you."

Hazel patted her handbag. "I just received it. Should I read it now?"

Eleanor nodded with unexpected vigor. "Please. I wrote it last night when my mind was clear. I might not say things as well now."

Hazel retrieved the envelope, noting the slight tremor in her own fingers. She opened it and unfolded a single sheet of stationery, the handwriting shaky but legible.

Hazel,

Max had a huge teenage crush on Mary. He would hide in her front garden and watch her. I confronted him once. He said he loved her. But it wasn't love. It was infatuation, possession even. He may have bullied Mary into hiding the money in the cottage for him.

I need you to know the whole truth before I join him.

Eleanor

Hazel's chest tightened. She folded the letter and slipped it back into its envelope.

Eleanor watched her, alert and searching. "You know about Max and Mary now. At first, it was harmless. He mooned all over her. He used to call them M & M, as in the chocolate buttons. The peanut variety came out that year, and there's no way I would remember that if Max hadn't killed Mary."

"Everything is so much more complicated than we thought," Hazel said.

Eleanor's eyes drifted to the painting on her wall—Mary's painting. "But you found the money in the little blue cottage of all places."

Hazel sat forward. "Eleanor, Max didn't rob the bank. We have proof that Mary and Cathy did."

A sharp intake of breath. "Cathy Robinson? Is that what you discovered in the tunnels?"

"Yes. They used a secret entrance from the tunnels that gave them direct access to the bank vault. But we think Max found out somehow."

Eleanor's fingers twisted the edge of her blanket. "He used to follow Mary everywhere. I told him it was wrong, but he'd give me that cold stare—the one that made me shut my mouth and scurry away."

Hazel suppressed a shudder. "So he could have seen Mary and Cathy the night of the heist."

"Possibly. About two weeks before her death, he became even more obsessed." Her face crumpled. "I should have warned Mary. She was so kind to me."

Hazel's throat tightened. "It wasn't your fault, Eleanor."

"But it was." Tears brimmed and slipped down her papery cheek. "Because I knew what Max was doing, and I did nothing. And then after she died, I helped him. I lied for him."

Hazel pulled a handkerchief from her pocket and gently wiped away her own tears.

"What happened the night Mary died, Eleanor?"

Eleanor closed her eyes, her breathing shallow. "He thought he could make Mary love him, but I believe she rejected him and laughed at him."

Eleanor's hands quaked. Hazel covered them with her own.

A cold knot formed in Hazel's stomach. "And Cathy? Do you think—"

"I don't know," Eleanor cut in. "We all thought she'd moved to the city."

"Did you know Mary and Cathy were in a relationship?" Hazel asked.

"What... How... But... she was dating Victor?"

"We think that was a diversion."

Eleanor recoiled against her chair. "Mary and Cathy? Together?" She shook her head in disbelief. "In Willowcroft? In 1954?"

Hazel nodded. "Yes, dear. We found evidence."

"Good heavens." Eleanor pressed her palm against her chest. "That sort of thing... Well, it wasn't discussed back then. People would have been scandalized." Her voice dropped to a whisper. "They'd have lost everything—their jobs, their homes, their standing in the community."

A thoughtful expression crossed Eleanor's face as she stared out the window. "Though I suppose it explains why Mary never seemed truly interested in any of the local boys. Victor always struck me as more of a companion than a sweetheart."

Hazel leaned in. "We found love letters with the bank money."

"Love letters?" Eleanor's eyebrows shot up.

"Beautiful ones. Cathy had quite a way with words." Hazel smiled. "But more than that, the letters detailed exactly how they broke into the bank."

Eleanor shook her head. "And to think, all these years, I believed it was Max. It was two women in love, hoping for a future."

"A future they never got to have," Hazel said.

Eleanor's expression darkened. "If Max discovered their relationship—and the money—" She stopped, her hand trembling as she reached for her water glass.

Hazel steadied the glass for her. "We think he might have been blackmailing them."

"Max was always greedy." Eleanor took a shaky sip. "Our parents favored him, but it was never enough. He always wanted more." She set the glass down with deliberate care. "If he knew about the money, he would have wanted it. And if Mary rejected him—"

"It would have crushed his pride," Hazel finished. "Especially if she laughed at him."

Eleanor's expression darkened. "Max couldn't handle rejection or humiliation."

"We think he might have killed Cathy too."

Eleanor's breath caught.

"We're speculating," Hazel assured her. "We haven't confirmed that the skeleton from the tunnels *is* Cathy or how they died. We may never know the full story."

"The not knowing is the hardest part." Eleanor wiped her tears. "But these days, no one would even notice two women in love, would they?"

Hazel smiled. "No. Things have changed for the better in that department."

"Good." Eleanor nodded firmly. "Love shouldn't have to hide in tunnels and letters." She glanced at Mary's painting, her expression softening. "Perhaps that's why I've always been drawn to this painting. There's something in those brushstrokes—a joy, despite everything."

Hazel followed her gaze to the canvas.

"Mary should have run away with Cathy when she had the chance," Eleanor said. "Away from this town, away from Max."

"Why do you think she stayed?"

Eleanor considered for a moment. "Mary always said Willowcroft had the perfect light for painting." A sad smile curved her lips. "She loved this town, despite its narrowness."

Hazel's heart twisted. "She sounds remarkable."

"She was." Eleanor's gaze turned inward. "And if Max killed her in a fit of jealousy and greed—" her voice hardened with sudden clarity, "—then I've protected a monster all these years."

"You were protecting yourself too," Hazel reminded her. "He threatened you."

"Yes, but I should have been braver." Eleanor folded her hands in her lap, her shoulders straightening despite her frail frame. "I'm glad the truth is finally coming out."

"It's never too late for truth," Hazel said.

Eleanor's expression steadied. "I'd like to make one more statement for the sheriff. Something official. For Mary and Cathy's sake."

"I'll arrange it," Hazel promised.

"Thank you." Eleanor reached for Hazel's hand again. "Thank you for not letting their story fade away."

Hazel squeezed her hand. "That's what friends do."

"Friends," Eleanor repeated with a small smile. "Mary would have liked you, Hazel. You share her same determination."

Chapter 27

Xander tugged at the hem of his hoodie as he sat in the green room of Waves of Willowcroft, bouncing his knee hard enough to shake the entire couch. His parents sat across from him, his dad, Ranger Dan Simmons, leaning back with his arms crossed, and his mom, Dr. Lauren Simmons, giving him a reassuring smile.

"You look like you're about to pass out," his dad said, inspecting him like a hiker about to topple off a cliff. "You sure you're okay, buddy?"

"I'm fine," Xander lied. His stomach had decided to audition for a gymnastics competition, but sure, totally fine.

His mom squeezed his hand. "You've already done the hard part—you wrote the set. Now you just have to read it."

"Yeah," Xander muttered, fidgeting with his glasses. "In front of the entire town."

Mrs. T entered the room, radiating calm, carrying a thermos of tea like it contained the key to the universe. Olivia was right behind her, grinning from ear to ear.

"Oh, dear," Mrs. T said, handing him a cup. "Nerves are perfectly natural. Even the best performers get the shakes."

Xander took a sip, inhaling the warm chamomile and honey. The only problem? His hands were shaking too much to hold the cup steady.

Olivia sat beside him, nudging him with her elbow. "You're going to kill it, Xander. The whole town is rooting for you."

"That doesn't help," he muttered. "If I bomb, that's all anyone will talk about until I graduate."

"That's true," Olivia said, ever unhelpful. "But they'll also remember if you nail it. Aim for that one."

The studio tech peeked in. "You're next, Xander."

His pulse tripled.

His mom smiled. "No matter what, we are so proud of you."

His dad nodded. "Yeah. And if anyone heckles you, I've got bear spray in the truck."

"Please don't bear spray the audience, Dad."

"I'm just saying. Options."

Mrs. T patted his arm. "Show them who you are, dear. That's all that matters."

Xander exhaled sharply, then stood. "Okay. Let's do this before I change my mind."

As he stepped toward the booth, Olivia gave him a final thumbs-up.

And then—he was on.

The familiar voice of DJ Rick Dawson crackled through the studio speakers, carrying its usual laid-back charm.

"All right, folks, it's time for a special segment. Waves of Willowcroft's first-ever Teen Comedy Night! We've got a fantastic lineup from all over Greater Willowcroft—Stonefield, Lakeview, Pinebrush—and representing right here in Willowcroft Township, we've got our very own tech whiz, Xander Simmons!"

A scattering of applause played from the soundboard as DJ Rick continued, his grin practically audible.

"Now, I gotta say—Xander's been making waves lately, and not just on our radio frequencies. If you've been following the latest town buzz, you know this kid's had a busy few weeks. But tonight, he's trading in mystery-solving for mic-dropping. So, Willowcroft, give it up for Xander!"

Xander took a shaky breath, patted his laptop, and stepped up to the mic.

Silence.

His mouth opened, then closed. The words... didn't come...

He cleared his throat, gripped the mic tighter, and tried again.

"So, last week, Dad took me camping."

He peeked through the sound booth window. His dad gave him a thumbs up.

Xander's shoulders dropped a notch. He continued.

"He's like, 'Son, let me teach you about the stars.' I'm thinking, great, I've got three astronomy apps for this. But he wants me to use this ancient star chart that looks like it was drawn by a caffeinated squirrel.

"Meanwhile, I'm getting notifications that my weather monitoring program is detecting a storm front. Dad's trying to find the North Star when I'm like, 'Hey, we should pack up—there's an eighty-nine point four percent chance of rain in twelve minutes.'

"He didn't believe me until the first drops hit.

"But the worst part about your dad being the park ranger is that everyone expects me to be this outdoorsy kid who can start fires with two sticks and track deer by their droppings. But the only tracking I do is with Python code, and the only fire I start is when I accidentally overclock my computer.

"And how about the whole thing in a small town where everyone knows your business before you do? Like, Mrs. Hubbard at the grocery store will ask me how my math test went before I've even gotten my grade back. I'm pretty sure she's hacked into the school's database. Actually, that would explain why her store's Wi-Fi is so suspiciously good...

"And don't get me started on how fast news travels here. I once Googled 'how to fix a bike chain,' and five minutes later, three different neighbors arrived with WD-40 and advice. I didn't even HAVE a bike problem—I was helping my friend code a bike repair app!

"But hey, at least I've got one thing going for me—I'm the only kid in town who can hack the swimming pool's PA system to play the *Jaws* theme when Mrs. Peters does her morning laps...

"Don't ask me about the dating thing. Try being the only computer nerd in a town where 'good boyfriend material' means knowing how to gut a fish. The closest I've gotten to romance was when Jenny Miller asked me to fix her phone. Turns out she wanted me to delete the evidence that she'd been texting Bobby Tucker. Thanks for the trust issues, Jenny.

"But the really wild thing is last month, Dad figured out I have useful skills. There was this lost hiker, right? Dad's out there with his maps and compass, and I'm just... tracking the guy's smartwatch GPS signal. Found him in ten minutes. He was at The Blarney Tap bar, by the way. Turns out he wasn't lost—he'd lied to his wife.

"So yeah, I might not be able to start a fire with two sticks, but I can write a program to calculate the optimal stick-rubbing velocity for maximum friction-based combustion. And sure, I can't track deer droppings, but I've got a drone that can spot a deer from half a mile away—at least until Mrs. Drummond's cat attacked it.

"I guess what I'm saying is, in a small town like Willowcroft, you either learn to embrace who you are, or you end up like that lost hiker—pretending to be something you're not and getting busted by a teenager with a laptop.

"Besides, Dad's coming around. Last week, he actually asked me to help him set up his trail cameras. Though I'm pretty sure he regrets it now that I've programmed them to play Rick Astley whenever they detect a raccoon..."

As the last line of Xander's set landed, the sound booth erupted into applause. Even DJ Rick—who'd probably heard more bad teen jokes in the last week than anyone should—grinned as he gave Xander a solid clap on the back.

"Give it up for Xander Simmons, folks! Our very own Willowcroft wonderkid. You can't teach timing like that!"

Xander let out a long breath. He'd done it.

As he peeled off his headphones, his mom and dad were waiting outside the booth, their smiles equal parts relief and pride.

"You were amazing!" his mom gushed, pulling him into a brief but enthusiastic hug.

His dad grinned. "Yeah. And for once, you impressed people without hacking anything."

Xander let out a breathless laugh. "I'll consider that progress."

Mrs. T reached for her phone. "Oh, the Knotty but Nice chat is in a tizzy, dear. You have fans."

Olivia smirked. "Peggy had the whole diner listening in. You're famous now."

Xander froze mid-step.

"The whole diner?"

"Yep. Better get used to signing autographs," Olivia teased, pushing open the station's front door.

The cool night air hit Xander's flushed face. The square was quiet, but the glow of the Swinging Spoon was warm and inviting across the way.

Through the glass windows, he saw half the town packed inside—Peggy, the Willow-Crafters, Lockie, Sheriff Stanton, Nick Bradley, even a few of his dad's ranger friends—all grinning, waiting.

As he stepped inside, the entire crowd erupted in cheers, the sound shaking the light fixtures.

"THERE HE IS!" Peggy hollered from behind the counter. The radio was still playing, though she'd lowered the volume from when she'd blasted Xander's performance through the speakers for everyone eating dinner.

Betty waved wildly from a booth. "Oh, that was delightful! You have the timing of a true performer!"

Mrs. Beasley clapped. "Oh, you had me in stitches! That bit about Mrs. Hubbard hacking the school database? Inspired."

Marjorie, sitting stiffly with her tea, gave a grudging nod. "Not terrible."

Xander rubbed the back of his neck, cheeks burning. "You, uh... you all heard it then?"

Peggy slammed a milkshake in front of him. "We had a listening party! You had 'em roaring, kid."

His dad clapped a firm hand on his shoulder. "Told you. Whole town's behind you."

His mom smiled, eyes crinkling. "You're a Willowcroft sensation."

Xander groaned, hiding his face in his hands. "Great. Now I'll never live this down."

Olivia snorted. "Nope. Never."

Mrs. T handed him a plate of fries. "You earned these, dear. And if you ever need help writing your next set, I'm sure the Knotty but Nice group chat would be delighted to assist."

Marjorie huffed. "Don't you dare drag us into this."

"Speak for yourself," Betty said, winking. "How about a romance joke next time?"

"Absolutely not," Xander said.

Across the diner, the radio played softly, fading into an ad break.

Peggy leaned against the counter, smirking. "So, superstar, how does it feel being Willowcroft's newest celebrity?"

Xander grabbed his milkshake and gave a dramatic sigh. "This isn't me."

As the diner erupted into another round of applause, Xander finally let himself smile.

Because, yeah.

That wasn't so bad after all.

Chapter 28

The following Saturday, the aroma of warm buttered toast hit Tammy's nose and the clamor of cutlery and chatter filled her ears as she, Wally, and Lockie entered the Swinging Spoon.

In a window booth, Olivia and Xander were deep in conversation. Mrs. Temperance sat opposite, fumbling through her knitting bag.

"Good morning, everyone," Peggy greeted them, pouring coffee into five cups. "Welcome to re-opening day. It's so nice to no longer have a crime scene in the basement."

The door to the diner swung open, and Officer Stanton entered, clutching a rolled-up newspaper under his arm. He approached the group with a nod of acknowledgment.

"Morning, folks," he greeted them, unfolding the newspaper and placing it on the table. "I wanted to drop by and thank you all for your help in solving this case. Your efforts have been invaluable."

"Of course, Sheriff," Olivia replied. "We were happy to do our part."

"However," Stanton continued, directing a stern glare around the table, "I must ask again that you refrain from involving yourselves in future investigations. You've done an incredible job, but we'd prefer if you kept to your day jobs and left the detective work to us professionals. I'm sure you understand."

He paused. "Promise me you won't cause any more trouble."

The team exchanged sheepish looks, a silent conversation passing between them.

"Understood," Wally said, his tone suggesting he wasn't being truthful.

"Good. Now, on a more positive note," Stanton said, "the bank's insurance at the time paid out. The company no longer operates, so the bank manager has donated the money to the mayor for the benefit of the whole town. Any ideas?"

The group fell thoughtful. Tammy was already brainstorming ways to improve her new community with the unexpected windfall.

"Also," Stanton added, "I wanted to inform you that we have cleared and opened all remaining crime scenes. Tammy and Lockie, you can now leave Wally's place and return home to the little blue cottage."

"Thanks, Sheriff," Tammy said with a smile, eager to settle back into her own space.

"I'll leave you to your breakfast."

Stanton walked away, leaving the team with the newspaper.

Tammy's eyes went to the headline: "Skeletal Remains Confirmed As Cathy Robinson." A faded photograph showed a smiling young woman.

"That's the picture Mrs. Robinson had in her living room," said Xander, addressing Mrs. T.

"We were right," Tammy said, her finger tracing the outline of Cathy's photograph. "The skeleton in the tunnels... it was her all along. She never made it to the city like everyone thought."

She scanned the article. "It says, 'DNA testing has confirmed the skeletal remains discovered by 'local amateur investigators'"—she looked up with a grin—"that's us—are those of Catherine 'Cathy' Robinson, long thought to have relocated to the city after the 1954 bank heist and the murder of Mary Collins."

She continued, summarizing the next part. "They got the DNA match from a hairbrush. Mrs. Robinson provided it; Cathy's brother, James, had kept it in a box with her things all these years."

Xander grimaced. "Keeping a hairbrush for seventy years... that's creepy."

"But smart," Wally countered. "Without it, we might never have identified the body."

"Remember what Mrs. Robinson said," Mrs. T said, turning to Xander. "Cathy's brother—Mrs. Robinson's husband—knew something was wrong all along. He was only a few years older than I was back then. He carried that loss his whole life, never knowing what happened to his sister."

Wally nodded. "All those years searching, and she was right beneath their feet."

Tammy found her place in the article. "There's no mention of how she died. Just that the remains were discovered near a 'bloodied rock outcropping' in the tunnels." The image of the damp, cloying darkness flickered in her mind.

Wally rubbed his chin. "So they *aren't* calling it foul play, maybe leaning toward an accident? We may never understand what happened down there."

"There's more. Mrs. Robinson has requested that once forensics release Cathy's remains, she wants her buried with Mary in the town cemetery."

"So they'll be together forever," Olivia said, her voice catching.

"And she hopes the town will rally around for Cathy's service the way they did for Mary," Tammy read. "She wants to give Cathy the farewell she never received."

"First Mary, and now Cathy," Mrs. Temperance said, dabbing at the corner of her eye with a tissue. "These poor girls deserved so much more."

"Those tunnels..." Xander shook his head. "I can't imagine dying there alone."

"She must have thought no one would ever find her," Tammy said, her hand finding Lockie's soft fur. "But we did. Her family knows the truth now."

"Mary's murder, Cathy's death, the bank heist... everything was connected," Wally said.

"The crime scenes are open again. We can go back to the tunnels for more clues," Olivia said.

"Agreed," Tammy said. "I'd love to explore them more. I hate to leave it so ambiguous." Tammy frowned. Novels always have neat endings, but there was nothing neat about this ending. "But I suppose some mysteries aren't meant to be fully solved."

Mrs. Temperance patted Tammy's hand. "You're a clever girl, dear. But even the best sleuths encounter dead ends."

Xander sat back in his chair, exhaling heavily. "We all want definitive answers. But we've done our best with the information we had."

Tammy's face lit up. "The tunnels! What if we opened them as a tourist attraction starting from my cottage? It would bring visitors to town."

"Not a bad idea," Wally said. "It would draw interest with the recent news coverage."

"We can use the bank money to create access points and trails. People would love exploring the clandestine history."

Olivia glowed at the idea. "That's brilliant! We can have plaques describing the town's history and stories of Mary, Cathy, and Max."

Peggy came by to clear their plates.

"The tours could end here at the Swinging Spoon's basement entrance," said Tammy.

"It would bring more business to the Spoon," Wally added with a grin.

Peggy beamed. "I love it! Something good needs to come from those tunnels."

"I think it's a lovely way to honor the past and move forward," said Mrs. Temperance.

"Count me in!" Olivia declared. "I'm sure I can uncover even more fascinating facts about Willowcroft's past for the tours. And I can sell the tickets at my store."

"An excellent plan," Mrs. Temperance agreed. "It seems our little mystery-solving group has brought some added value to this town."

"About the tunnels," Xander said, pulling his laptop from his messenger bag. "I've been working on something."

Tammy scooted closer as Xander's screen flickered to life, and a crude outline of Willowcroft's streets appeared, overlaid with jagged red lines snaking beneath them.

"Is this what I think it is?" Olivia asked.

"The tunnels." Xander tapped a few keys, zooming in on the section beneath the town square. "I took measurements and matched everything with the streets above ground."

Tammy leaned forward, coffee forgotten. "It's not complete."

"That's the problem." Xander scratched his head. "We only explored a fraction of what's there."

"Are you suggesting there's more to discover?" Mrs. Temperance asked.

"Much more." Xander pointed to several places where the tunnels formed partial geometric shapes.

Tammy's skin tingled. "The sheriff has the original map as evidence, right?"

"Yeah, but we still have Mrs. T's photos." Xander rubbed his neck.

"Can you send them to me?" The question burst from Tammy's lips.

"You planning something?" Wally asked, an eyebrow raised.

Tammy shrugged. "Maybe. I've got this theory about the symbols carved into the walls. They might be more than just markers."

"You're starting your own deciphering project." A smile spread across Xander's face before his fingers flew across the keys, and Tammy's phone vibrated with the files.

"Someone has to figure out what those symbols mean." Tammy stroked Lockie, who purred in her lap. "And the Sheriff's Department won't dedicate resources to it."

"Tammy," Mrs. Temperance said, her voice gentle but firm, "the sheriff specifically asked us to stay out of trouble."

"Researching isn't trouble." Tammy sipped her coffee.

"Until you find something interesting," Olivia said.

Xander closed his laptop. "There's something else. Some tunnels don't appear on the original map at all."

The table fell silent.

"Why would someone hide tunnels on a tunnel map?" Wally asked.

"That's what I want to know." Xander slid his laptop back into his bag. "I'll send you everything, Tammy. Just—"

"Don't go down there alone," they all said in unison.

Tammy raised her hands in surrender. "I hear you." *But I'll probably ignore you.*

"We haven't discovered the exact details of how they got into the bank, only that they used the tunnels," said Olivia.

"So the tunnels are our next adventure?" asked Mrs. T.

Wally drained his coffee cup. "I'm in. Better than sitting around wondering what else is hiding in this town's history."

Xander grinned. "Mapping isn't sleuthing either. It's science. Besides, if we are going to turn it into a tourist attraction, we need to understand what we are dealing with."

"Good point," said Olivia.

Tammy stroked Lockie. "What other mysteries does this town hold?"

"Only time will tell," Mrs. Temperance smiled.

"I guess we'll always be amateur sleuths at heart," said Olivia.

"Speak for yourself," Xander said with a chuckle. "I'm retiring from this line of work."

The team laughed.

Olivia gave Xander's arm a teasing punch. "No, you're not."

Xander feigned pain. "Of course I'm not; I never want to stop solving mysteries."

Mrs. Temperance's coffee cup landed on the table with a clink. "This case shows why understanding our past is so vital. The events of yesterday shape our today, whether we realize it or not."

She gazed out the window, her expression thoughtful. "Mary and Cathy's story remained buried for decades, affecting generations. Greg was still carrying his grandfather's perceived shame as if it was his own."

"And it warped him," said Olivia. "He sent threatening letters, attacked Wally—all to protect a reputation that didn't even need saving. That's why, if we don't understand our history, we stay trapped in it. Genealogy helps us see the patterns and truths... and break the cycle."

"Speaking of which, dear," Mrs. Temperance turned to her with a curious expression, "I've always wondered how you developed such a passion for family histories. It's not a common interest for someone your age."

Olivia laughed, a hint of self-consciousness in her expression. "Let's just say my mother learned a hard lesson about assumptions." She stirred her coffee. "When I was sixteen, Mother applied to the Daughters of the

American Revolution. With a maiden name like Tallmadge, she was certain we had revolutionary blood."

"Oh my," Mrs. Temperance's brows lifted.

"Her country club friends were all members, and she appointed herself the family historian overnight," Olivia continued. "She kept going on about how our ancestors dined with George Washington."

Tammy leaned forward. "But they didn't?"

"Not even close," Olivia said. "I started researching for a school project and discovered our branch of Tallmadges weren't patriots at all—they weren't even loyalists. They were tenant farmers who worked someone else's land in rural Pennsylvania and never owned property or fought in a war."

"That's not what Mother was expecting," Wally guessed.

"It gets worse," Olivia continued. "I traced our actual lineage to a John Tallmadge who came to America in the 1820s—not on a grand ship, but as an indentured servant who couldn't read or write. He signed his contracts with an 'X.' And the real kicker? He changed his name when he arrived because he was running from debts in England—our family name isn't even really Tallmadge."

"Wait a minute," Xander perked up. "Tallmadge? As in Benjamin Tallmadge? George Washington's spymaster? The guy who ran the Culper Ring during the Revolution?"

Olivia gave a rueful smile. "The very one. Mother believed we were direct descendants."

"That would have been perfect for you!" Xander exclaimed. "Claiming espionage was in your blood. The genealogist with spy ancestry solving cold cases. What a missed opportunity."

"I'll have to rely on my own talents rather than hereditary spy genes," Olivia laughed.

"Your mother must have been mortified by the truth," Mrs. Temperance observed.

"The DAR application disappeared overnight," Olivia confirmed with a laugh. "Mother's friends stopped asking about our 'distinguished lineage.' But I was hooked. I discovered our real ancestors were far more interesting than the fictional revolutionaries she'd imagined—they were ordinary people who survived through difficult circumstances. Our family tree is full of seamstresses, coal miners, and farmhands—not a war hero or society figure to be found."

"The lineage of honest work is nothing to be ashamed of," Mrs. Temperance said.

"I agree," Olivia said. "But Mother still winces whenever genealogy comes up at dinner parties. I discovered how easy it is to believe family myths without checking facts. Our histories aren't always what we imagine them to be—but they're always worth knowing, even the uncomfortable parts."

"Especially the uncomfortable parts," Mrs. Temperance added. "The past needs to be understood, not buried. Only then can we truly forgive it and move forward."

Tammy glanced at the newspaper still folded on the booth seat beside her. Cathy's photo peeked out from the corner. Not a revolutionary or a spy—just a girl whose story had been lost in the dark. But now she was part of their history too. Not forgotten. Not buried anymore.

The team nodded in agreement, a moment of shared understanding passing between them.

As they left the diner, Lockie meowed, rubbing against Tammy's leg. Tammy smiled, giving him an affectionate scratch behind the ears. A commotion across the square made her pause.

"What's that?" she asked, pointing toward The Retro Reel cinema next to the radio station.

The marquee lights were flashing on one by one, illuminating a new display:

"OCEAN'S 8 – ONE NIGHT ONLY"
IN HONOR OF MARY & CATHY
FUNDRAISER FOR WILLOWCROFT PRIDE – COMING NEXT
JUNE

"When did they organize that?" Xander asked.

"Let's check it out," Olivia suggested, already stepping off the curb.

The group crossed the square, drawn by the growing buzz of activity. A small crowd had gathered outside the theater. Bev from the Sheriff's Department and Maxine, the librarian, were setting up a folding table adorned with rainbow-colored bunting beneath the marquee.

Lockie darted ahead, fascinated by the colorful streamers fluttering in the breeze. He pounced, entangling himself in a loop of loose rainbow bunting.

"Lockie!" Tammy rushed forward as the cat twisted, wrapping himself even tighter in the festive garland.

"I've got him," Wally said, extracting the squirming bundle of fur. "He wants to help decorate."

Maxine glanced up from arranging flyers on the table. "The amateur detectives! Just the people we wanted to see." She gestured toward the marquee. "What do you think? We thought it would be a fitting tribute."

"It's perfect," Tammy said, cradling Lockie after Wally freed him from the bunting. "They would have loved it."

"The town council approved emergency funding for a special screening," Bev explained. "All proceeds will go to the new Willowcroft Pride initiative. We're calling it 'Let's Celebrate the Story They Never Got to Tell.'"

A handwritten sign propped against the ticket booth read exactly that, the rainbow letters bright against the white poster board.

"They were bold, brilliant, and underestimated," Olivia said. "If that's not *Ocean's 8* material, I don't know what is."

"Think they'd be flattered by the comparison?" Xander asked, his expression thoughtful.

"I think they'd be amazed anyone remembered at all," said Mrs. Temperance.

Only in Willowcroft would a decades-old unsolved heist earn you a commemorative screening.

Sheriff Stanton emerged from the lobby doors, a roll of tape in one hand and a staple gun in the other. His usual gruffness had softened into something almost reverent.

"Sign keeps drooping on the left," he muttered, securing the rainbow banner above the table with practiced precision. He gave Bev a nod. "You said level, and level it is."

Tammy blinked in surprise. "Sheriff Stanton? You helped organize this?"

He gave a small shrug. "Didn't feel right not to. I viewed this case as black and white. Turns out, I missed all the color."

Mrs. Temperance pressed a hand to her chest. "Sheriff, that might be the most poetic thing I've ever heard you say."

"Don't get used to it," he grumbled—but there was a smile tugging at the corner of his mouth.

Someone flipped the switch on the ticket booth, bathing the sidewalk in soft golden light. Around them, the townspeople of Willowcroft gathered, eager to honor two women whose story remained unknown for too long.

Tammy held Lockie close, watching as someone taped a black-and-white photo of Mary and Cathy to the booth window. In that moment, she knew that while some details might remain unsolved, the most important truth had been uncovered. Mary and Cathy's story would never be forgotten again.

Something shifted inside her. She'd come to Willowcroft to regroup after her best friend and boyfriend had conspired against her, tanking both her trust and her book reviews. But she'd found more than peace. The town's tangled history, its secrets, and unsolved mysteries were the ideal fodder to stir her imagination in a fresh direction.

Cozy mysteries.

She patted Lockie. Surrounded by people who baked pies and unearthed long-forgotten tunnels, she had everything she needed: real history, real characters, and real inspiration.

After weeks of disruptions, they were free to return to a normal routine. Well... they hadn't had time to establish one yet. But she wanted one!

"Let's go home, buddy." Time to truly call Willowcroft and the little blue cottage home. "Or... we could explore *our* tunnels."

Chapter 29

Tammy faced a puzzle of faded ink and torn edges through the screen of her cell phone.

"This map led Cathy and Mary to the back entrance of the bank. It has to be able to get us there too, Lockie." She tilted the yellowed paper toward her beam. Lockie meowed in protest at her feet, his tail swishing against the dirty floor of the underground passage.

"I know, I know. Mother would have a fit if she knew what I was doing." Tammy twisted the flashlight between her fingers. "You're always so reckless, Tamantha," she mimicked in the high, clipped tone she reserved for her mother's voice in her head.

The love letters had solved the seventy-year-old bank heist mystery and revealed a network of tunnels beneath the town. Some of those tunnels ran under Tammy's newly acquired property—making them hers, at least temporarily.

Lockie stared at her with unblinking eyes. "I want to have them all to myself before we open them up for tourists."

She retraced their steps from when they discovered the entrance in Tammy's field. She made it through the spot they found the skeleton, a tiny piece of crime scene tape left wedged behind a rock.

Using Xander's town overlay map Tammy followed the path to where the bank should be and to the faded image of a roulette wheel on a door.

"This matches the symbol here," she said to Lockie, pointing at a circular mark on the map surrounded by annotations. The symbol didn't explicitly indicate it led to the bank, but given what she knew about Cathy and Mary's heist, Tammy's writer's instinct told her she was on the right track.

The door refused to budge when she pushed against it. Decades of disuse had sealed it more effectively than any lock.

Maybe I should have brought the others...

But I want to be the first. I'm not ready to share yet.

Tammy braced her shoulder against the wood and shoved. Nothing.

This calls for some improvisation. Good thing I came prepared.

She rummaged through her pack and pulled out the small crowbar she'd brought along—a precaution proving its worth. Wedging it into the gap between door and frame, she leveraged it with all her strength. The wood groaned in protest.

"Come on," she grunted, applying more pressure. Lockie retreated several steps.

With a splintering crack, the door gave way. Tammy stumbled forward, catching herself before she fell. Debris shot upward in a dry cloud, dancing in the single beam as it illuminated a scene frozen in time.

Gambling tables stood like sentinels in the darkness, their green felt covers dulled by age. Playing cards lay scattered across the floor, their once-bold colors now faded to ghosts of spades and diamonds. Overturned chairs suggested a hasty departure, while empty bottles stood in silent rows along a makeshift bar. The smell of time forgotten filled the air.

"Goodness," Tammy whispered. Her fingers itched for her notebook, already composing lines for a future novel. "Lockie, we've found the speakeasy."

The cat padded into the room, his paws leaving delicate prints on the floor as he investigated this unfamiliar territory.

Tammy moved deeper into the room, her light catching the glint of tarnished poker chips and the dull sheen of an ancient brass ashtray overflowing with cigarette butts preserved by the dry air. She turned over a playing card—the queen of hearts.

"They touched this," she said, thinking of Cathy and Mary. "They stood right here."

For a moment, phantom sounds of a jazz band played, glasses clinked, laughter hushed, and bets whispered.

Lockie jumped onto one of the gambling tables and sniffed at an empty martini glass. "Right under everyone's noses. Based on Xander's map and the Robinsons' house, the secret bank entrance has to be here." *Was the bank involved with the speakeasy? That doesn't sound ethical.*

She consulted the map again.

Tammy zoomed in on the map, squinting at the faded markings. The roulette wheel symbol matched the one carved into the door she'd forced open, but beneath it, additional symbols surrounded a roughly sketched shelf. An old-fashioned key, three dice showing threes, and a wine glass.

Scribbled beside them were the words: One for the banker, two for the bootlegger, three for the law.

A puzzle.

She turned her attention to the heavy velvet curtain covering the back wall. Dust billowed as she yanked it aside, revealing wooden shelves stacked with forgotten bottles of liquor, their labels peeling and the glass fogged with age.

"There's got to be some kind of door. But where?"

Her writer's mind filled with possibilities—a false book that triggered a mechanism, a candlestick that needed to be turned, a specific sequence of bottles to be pressed.

"If I were writing this scene," she told Lockie, who watched her with casual interest, "I'd make it something clever but not too obvious."

She began running her fingers along the edges of the shelves, feeling for anything unusual.

Lockie leaped onto the lowest shelf, knocking over a bottle that clinked against another. Tammy's breath hitched. A faint, mechanical click echoed in the quiet.

Heart pounding, she grabbed the bottle and inspected it. The glass was smooth and cool like the others, but when she lifted it again, the same soft click sounded beneath her fingers.

"A lever," she whispered. Tammy stepped closer and read what was left of their labels.

Some bore handwritten tags, their faded ink scrawled in careful cursive: Lawman's Last Call; Banker's Reserve; Bootlegger's Gold.

Tammy smirked. One for the banker, two for the bootlegger, three for the law.

This had to be the sequence.

She hesitated for a moment, then reached for Banker's Reserve and lifted it.

Click.

She exhaled and moved to Bootlegger's Gold. After lifting it, the shelf shifted slightly. Something behind it was unlocking.

Lockie crouched low, his tail flicking as he watched.

Her heart hammered in her chest. What if she triggered something other than a door? What if the tunnel gave way entirely? She hesitated, her fingers trembling over the final bottle. Too late to back out now.

She reached for Lawman's Last Call and lifted it off the shelf.

A low groan of gears shifting broke the silence.

Tammy took a step back.

The entire middle section of the shelving creaked, then jerked forward an inch.

She pressed her hands against the edges and pulled. *This is better than the bookstore's door.*

The panels slid apart with a theatrical flourish worthy of the best mystery novels or one of Olivia's impromptu performances. A hidden door behind a secret door. The craftsmanship was impeccable; even after seventy years, the mechanism worked with only the slightest resistance. More than functional, it was made to impress.

With a slow, reluctant groan, the shelf swung open on concealed hinges, revealing walls of safety deposit boxes.

Her pulse kicked up. She exhaled.

Cathy and Mary had stood here all those years ago, staring at the same boxes. This wasn't a tunnel. It was the bank itself. And with Cathy being the housekeeper, she would have cleaned the vault and seen its cash room.

Lockie padded inside first, tail high.

Tammy followed, stepping across the threshold with a sense of awe.

"Well," she murmured, "we've discovered how Cathy and Mary pulled off the best bank heist of all time. It only took seventy years for someone to figure it out."

"Good thing it's a weekend, or we may have gotten caught," she whispered to Lockie. "Olivia will lose her mind when she sees this."

Lockie crept along the wall, sniffing the fake boxes before giving a dismissive sneeze.

"Yes, they'll be furious I came here alone." She aimed her flashlight deeper into the vault. "But once they see it, how can they stay mad?"

A loud crack echoed from somewhere behind them.

Tammy whirled around, her heart leaping to her throat.

Another crack followed, then a low rumble that seemed to come from the walls themselves.

"This is bad." She closed the clandestine door and grabbed her backpack. "Lockie, time to go."

The cat bolted past her as the rumbling grew louder. He'd clearly voted for "get out" over "explore further."

Debris rained from the ceiling.

Tammy sprinted through the speakeasy.

The floor vibrated beneath her feet.

The noise swelled to a thunderous roar.

She burst through the door with the roulette wheel.

A deafening crash sounded behind her.

The force knocked her forward onto her knees.

When the air cleared, Tammy peered back. A wall of fallen rock and dirt now blocked the tunnel—as if the speakeasy had never existed.

Her breath came in sharp gasps. "That was close."

She stared at the collapse, the implications sinking in.

The bank's back entrance was gone—sealed off for good.

The physical evidence of how Cathy and Mary had pulled off their heist was locked away again.

Lockie circled back to her, meowing insistently.

"You're right." Tammy pushed herself to her feet, brushing dirt from her jeans. "We need to get out of here before more collapses."

She glanced one last time at the wall of debris, then turned and followed Lockie toward the exit. Her finger brushed against something in her pocket—the playing card she'd picked up from the speakeasy floor: the queen of hearts. A small souvenir from a place no one else would see.

A secret of her own.

"Maybe this is how it's supposed to be," she told Lockie as they navigated the winding tunnel. "Some mysteries aren't meant to be understood."

The others would want to know what she found. But without access to the speakeasy and the bank entrance, what proof did she have? Her word. A single card.

The truth about how Cathy and Mary had robbed the bank would remain between her, Lockie, and the ghosts of two women who had pulled off the perfect crime.

She quickened her pace as another distant rumble sounded from somewhere in the tunnel network. So much for their tourist attraction. Getting out alive seemed the highest priority.

EPILOGUE

Olivia stacked the new releases onto the front display, her fingers lingering on the spines as she counted inventory.

The front door swung open. Postmaster Glen Taylor strode in, clutching a small package. "Morning, Olivia. Personal delivery today."

She took the box and studied the unfamiliar Michigan return address. The weight and dimensions screamed "book," though she couldn't recall ordering anything.

Behind the counter, she sliced through the packaging tape. The hardcover slipped free: *Bootleggers and Bandits: The Michaels Family in Prohibition Michigan.*

"Of course." She'd ordered this during their investigation, but it materialized weeks too late. The Michaels connection had turned out to be nothing more than a red herring.

She cracked open the spine, planning to skim, but names leaped from the pages: Michaels, Grey, Walsh.

Words burned into her vision as she devoured page after page. The families' web of crime stretched far beyond bootlegging. "Business arrangements" and "mutual interests" littered the text, spanning decades before and after Prohibition. Dark deeds lurked beneath the veneer of respectable family histories.

If Elaine read this... no wonder she was careful about what she shared.

Olivia's hand stilled over a photograph. Three men stared back at her: Clark Michaels, Samuel Grey, and Victor Walsh.

The caption pierced through her chest: *Last photo taken before a feud over bank heist rumors tore the families apart.*

Ready to uncover the whole truth?

You've followed the team as they pieced together the clues, but some things were merely assumptions... **What *really* happened in 1954?**

Get the full, unvarnished story in my **exclusive FREE bonus novella!**

Step into the daily lives of those who lived it, including Mary Collins, Cathy Robinson, Victor Walsh, Max and Eleanor Cross, and even cameos from four-year-olds Hazel, Betty, and Marjorie! Witness the events as they unfold.

Sign up for my VIP Reader Newsletter today and I'll send you *Love, Loss & Loot* instantly!

Read your free novella now.

As a subscriber, you'll be the first to hear about new books, get access to exclusive content, have access to subscriber only puzzles pages and more.

Do you want to know more about the fued?

Can the tunnels be saved to become a museum?

Pick up

Podcasts, Pretenders & Pumpkins

today!

Chapter One

Crimson and gold leaves blanketed the roadside. Rowe Harvey's rental car sprayed a swath of them into the air as she swerved to a halt outside Willowcroft's Town Hall, a long-haired whirlwind determined to tear apart the town's carefully polished veneer.

She stepped out. The wind yanked at her trench coat. The storybook scene made her jaw clench. Too artificial. Too rehearsed.

Banners proclaiming "Willowcroft's Spooktacular Halloween Festival" flapped between lampposts with grinning skull decorations. Orange and purple bunting draped across storefronts. The air smelled of sugar and apples.

Thomas Berry from the *Willowcroft Gazette* approached with a broad smile, his tie patterned with tiny bats. "Ms. Harvey, welcome to Willowcroft." His handshake crushed her fingers. "I'm sure you'll find our history quite... invigorating."

"Cut the pleasantries." She adjusted the recorder in her hand, thumb hovering over the record button. "Where's the action?"

He shrugged and gestured toward the cluster of awnings nestled between flame-colored maples. "Right this way." He took off with a skip. "Olivia's bookstore is where I suggest you start."

Rowe scanned from Sweet Crumbs bakery's towering pies to Bookworm Haven's quaint displays and the Swinging Spoon diner's flashing neon. *Every inch screams rural perfection. But two murders and a bank heist tell a different story.* Beneath Willowcroft's facade lurked secrets only she knew to search for. The trail had led her here months ago.

Her true crime podcast about the Prohibition-era tunnels and seventy-year-old money trail would captivate her listeners, but Rowe pursued another goal entirely. Something personal she kept to herself.

Her feet pounded the cobblestones across the square. Thomas huffed behind her.

"What do you think of our town?" he asked when he finally caught up outside the bookstore.

"No shortage of real news elsewhere," she replied, fixating on Mrs. Hubbard's Cupboard grocery store painted in garish purple across the street. "I didn't abandon an election scandal for recipes and photo contests."

Fallen leaves spiraled around Rowe's boots. She gripped her lapels, squared her shoulders. Thomas's eager grin faltered.

"I'm here for the real story." Her fingers drummed against her recorder. "The truth behind this town's skeletons. Not the glossy brochure version."

She pushed through the bookstore's door without waiting for his response.

A woman with glasses and a cardigan looked up from behind the counter. "Hello! Welcome to the Bookworm Haven. Are you here for the museum preview?"

Rowe pressed record and thrust her microphone forward. "Rowe Harvey. True crime podcaster. You must be Olivia."

The woman's eyes widened. "Yes, that's me. I'm—"

"The owner of Bookworm Haven and ticket vendor for the tunnel museum," Rowe leaned forward. "Tell me about those tunnels. How did they stay hidden for so long?"

Olivia blinked twice. "Well, I suppose they were well-concealed. We didn't even know they existed until—"

"Until you and your friends solved Mary Collins' murder." Rowe studied the tiny flinch in Olivia's expression. "Walk me through how that happened."

Olivia's fingers straightened a stack of bookmarks on the counter. "It's quite a story, actually. It started this past summer when Tammy moved to town and found a threatening letter in her cottage attic."

"The little blue cottage where the money was eventually found."

"Yes, exactly." Olivia's eyebrow rose. "Tammy brought me the letter, and soon our little group formed to investigate. We connected it to Mary Collins' unsolved murder from seventy years ago, a classic locked room mystery."

A family entered the shop, the bell above the door jingling. Rowe's foot tapped against the wooden floor as Olivia excused herself. *Convenient interruption.* She eyed the flyers by the register advertising the museum courtesy bus while Olivia explained the schedule to the customers.

When the family left with their purchases, Rowe pounced. "The murder led you to the bank heist?"

"In a roundabout way," Olivia's shoulders relaxed. "While investigating Mary's death, we discovered she was somehow connected to the unsolved bank robbery that happened three weeks before her murder. No one had ever made that connection before."

"And your team?" Rowe prompted. "What made a bookseller, a..." She made a show of checking her notes, though she'd memorized the details. "...a retired detective, a tech specialist, and a town gossip qualified to solve what police couldn't for seventy years?"

Olivia's jaw tightened. "Mrs. Temperance is not a gossip. She's a local matriarch with invaluable knowledge about Willowcroft." She inhaled deeply. "And we each brought something unique: Wally's investigative experience, Xander's technical skills, my research abilities specializing in genealogy, and Tammy's writer perspective."

"Convenient," Rowe said. *Too convenient.* "So you solved the murder, then went hunting for the missing money?"

"Once we identified Max Cross as Mary's killer, yes. We figured he must have known where the bank money was hidden." Olivia's eyes brightened. "That search led us to discover the tunnels under Willowcroft, originally built during Prohibition, and to Cathy Robinson's skeleton."

"Mary's lover and accomplice in the heist," Rowe stated flatly.

"Yes." Olivia's voice softened. "They stumbled upon the vault entrance and stole the money but they didn't get the happy ending they'd hoped for."

"And how exactly did you find the money? After seventy years, it seems remarkably convenient."

Olivia hesitated before answering. "Max Cross's grandson, Nathan, had notes from his grandfather's dementia ramblings. They led us back to Tammy's cottage, where the money had been hidden under the attic floorboards all along."

"The cottage where Mary was murdered," Rowe said. "Poetic justice."

"I suppose you could say that." Olivia shifted her weight from one foot to the other.

"And now you've turned tragedy into tourism." Rowe jerked her chin toward the museum flyers. "Tell me about the logistics. How does this operation work?"

Olivia's shoulders dropped. "We've arranged a courtesy bus." She pointed out the window where a vintage-styled bus idled by the curb. "It takes visitors from here to the museum entrance by Tammy's cottage. The tour goes through the safe portions of the tunnels and ends at the Swinging Spoon diner back in town."

"Efficient," Rowe conceded, eyeing the bus. "And who does what at this museum?"

"Tammy, Wally, and Xander lead the tours," Olivia explained. "They share different perspectives based on their involvement in solving the case.

Mrs. Temperance manages the main exhibition room where we've displayed historical artifacts and the story timeline."

"And your role?"

"I sell the tickets here and maintain the historical documentation." Olivia gestured to a display of books about Prohibition and local history arranged near the counter.

"I'll be speaking with all of them." Rowe slipped her recorder into her pocket and angled toward the door. "Your local charm has been... illuminating."

"I hope you enjoy your time in Willowcroft," Olivia called after her, her voice pitching higher as Rowe headed for the exit.

Outside, Rowe fixed on the courtesy bus loading passengers. The driver, a heavyset man with ruddy cheeks, chatted with passengers. *Perfect source for town gossip.*

As the bus pulled away, Rowe's fingers curled into fists. The operation ran with precision. A seamless blend of history and entertainment. But beneath Willowcroft's picture-perfect surface lurked secrets she intended to expose. Not just the ones about Mary Collins and Cathy Robinson that everyone packaged for tourists, but the ones still buried deep in the town's consciousness.

I'm the trick to this town's Halloween treat.

Are you loving the Willowcoft Cozy Mystery Series?
Why don't you leave a review to help other readers find it!

Scan the QR code to write a review for
Skeletons, Secrets & Speakeasies.

www.ingramcontent.com/pod-product-compliance
Lightning Source LLC
Chambersburg PA
CBHW020514120726
47904CB00003B/827